"You are a dead man."

"Yeah, well, everybody dies sooner or later." He was heading south on 95, and grateful she'd stopped swearing at him.

"If you want to live to see another sunrise, pull this excuse for a car over, uncuff me and let me go."

"Go where? Back to your apartment?"

"That's my problem, not yours."

"Not anymore, sister. I take it personal when someone shoots at me. Since you seem to be the reason why, I'll be keeping you for a while until I get this figured out. You should be grateful."

"Oh, I should be grateful? You broke into my apartment, knocked me around, busted up my things and have me cuffed to a door handle."

"That's right. If I hadn't, you'd probably be lying in that apartment right now, with a bullet in your head.... Somebody wants you dead, sugar."

Dear Reader,

Merry Christmas, Happy Holidays of all sorts and welcome to another fabulous month's worth of books here at Intimate Moments. And here's a wonderful holiday gift for you: *Captive Star*, the newest book from bestselling, award-winning and just plain incredibly talented author Nora Roberts. The next of THE STARS OF MITHRA miniseries, this book has Nora's signature sizzle and spark, all wrapped up in a compellingly suspenseful plot about a couple on the run—handcuffed together!

We've got another miniseries "jewel" for you, too: *The Taming of Reid Donovan*, the latest in Marilyn Pappano's SOUTHERN KNIGHTS series. There's a twist in this one that I think will really catch you by surprise. Susan Sizemore debuts at Silhouette with *Stranger by Her Side*, a book as hot and steamy as its setting.

And then there are our Christmas books, three tantalizing tales of holiday romance. *One Christmas Knight*, by Kathleen Creighton, features one of the most memorable casts of characters I've ever met. Take one gentlemanly Southern trucker, one about-to-deliver single mom, the biggest snowstorm in a generation, put them together and what do you get? How about a book you won't be able to put down? Rebecca Daniels is back with *Yuletide Bride*, a secret child story line with a Christmas motif. And finally, welcome brand-new author Rina Naiman, whose *A Family for Christmas* is a warm and wonderful holiday debut.

Enjoy—and the very happiest of holidays to you and yours.

Leslie J. Wainger
Senior Editor and Editorial Coordinator

Please address questions and book requests to:
Silhouette Reader Service
U.S.: 3010 Walden Ave., P.O. Box 1325, Buffalo, NY 14269
Canadian: P.O. Box 609, Fort Erie, Ont. L2A 5X3

Nora Roberts

CAPTIVE STAR

The Stars of Mithra

INTIMATE MOMENTS

Published by Silhouette Books

America's Publisher of Contemporary Romance

SILHOUETTE BOOKS

ISBN 0-373-07823-4

CAPTIVE STAR

This edition published by arrangement with Harlequin Books S.A.

® and TM are trademarks of Harlequin Books S.A., used under license.
Trademarks indicated with ® are registered in the United States Patent
and Trademark Office, the Canadian Trade Marks Office and in other
countries.

Printed in U.S.A.

Books by Nora Roberts

McGregor Series
Playing the Odds SE #225
Tempting Fate SE #235
All the Possibilities SE #247
One Man's Art SE #259
For Now, Forever SE #361

The O'Hurleys!
The Last Honest Woman SE #451
Dance to the Piper SE #463
Skin Deep SE #475
Without a Trace SE #625

The Calhoun Women
Courting Catherine RS #801
A Man for Amanda D #649
For the Love of Lilah SE #685
Suzanna's Surrender IM #397
Megan's Mate IM #745

The Donovan Legacy
Captivated SE #768
Entranced SE #774
Charmed SE #780

Cordina's Royal Family
Affaire Royale IM #142
Command Performance IM #198
The Playboy Prince IM #212

Those Wild Ukrainians
Taming Natasha SE #583
Luring a Lady SE #709
Falling for Rachel SE #810
Convincing Alex SE #872
Waiting for Nick SE #1088

Night Tales
Night Shift IM #365
Night Shadow IM #373
Nightshade IM #529
Night Smoke IM #595

The MacKade Brothers
The Return of
Rafe MacKade IM #631
The Pride of
Jared MacKade SE #1000
The Heart of
Devin MacKade IM #697
The Fall of
Shane MacKade SE #1022

The Stars of Mithra
Hidden Star IM #811
Captive Star IM #823

Silhouette Books
Silhouette Christmas Stories 1986
"Home for Christmas"
Silhouette Summer Sizzlers 1989
"Impulse"
Birds, Bees and Babies 1994
"The Best Mistake"
Jingle Bells, Wedding Bells 1994
"All I Want for Christmas"

NORA ROBERTS

is one of Silhouette Books' most popular and prolific authors, as well as a *New York Times* bestselling author in both hardcover and paperback. Nora was the first author inducted into the Romance Writers of America Hall of Fame and has received awards for her fiction, her creativity, her sales and her contribution to the genre. She has received lifetime achievement awards from the Romance Writers of America, Waldenbooks and *Romantic Times* magazine, and bestselling title and series awards from booksellers, readers and peers.

Nora Roberts is a consummate storyteller. She is known for her humor, creativity and willingness to take chances. Nora's commitment to her characters, to her writing and, most especially, to her readers, has earned her fans all over the world.

To independent women

Chapter 1

He'd have killed for a beer. A big, frosty mug filled with some dark import that would go down smoother than a woman's first kiss. A beer in some nice, dim, cool bar, with a ball game on the tube and a few other stool-sitters who had an interest in the game gathered around.

While he staked out the woman's apartment, Jack Dakota passed the time fantasizing about it.

The foamy head, the yeasty smell, the first gulping swallow to beat the heat and slake the thirst. Then the slow savoring, sip by sip, that assured a man all would be right with the world if only politicians and lawyers would debate the inevitable conflicts over a cold one at a local pub while a batter faced a count of three and two.

It was a bit early for drinking, at just past one in

the afternoon, but the heat was so huge, so intense and the cooler full of canned sodas just didn't have quite the same punch as a cold, foamy beer.

His ancient Oldsmobile didn't run to amenities like air-conditioning. In fact, its amenities were pathetically few, except for the pricey, earsplitting stereo he'd installed in the peeling faux-leather dash. The stereo was worth about double the blue book on the car, but a man had to have music. When he was on the road, he enjoyed turning it up to scream and belting them out with the Beatles or the Stones.

The muscle-flexing V-8 engine under the dented gutter-gray hood was tuned as meticulously as a Swiss watch, and got Jack where he wanted to go, fast. Just now the engine was at rest, and as a concession to the quiet neighborhood in northwest Washington, D.C., he had the CD player on murmur while he hummed along with Bonnie Raitt.

She was one of his rare bows to music after 1975.

Jack often thought he'd been born out of his own time. He figured he'd have made a pretty good knight. A black one. He liked the straightforward philosophy of might for right. He'd have stood with Arthur, he mused, tapping his fingers on the steering wheel. But he'd have handled Camelot's business his own way. Rules complicated things.

He'd have enjoyed riding the West, too. Hunting down desperadoes without all the nonsense of paperwork. Just track 'em down and bring 'em in.

Dead or alive.

These days, the bad guys hired a lawyer, or the

state gave them one, and the courts ended up apologizing to them for the inconvenience.

We're terribly sorry, sir. Just because you raped, robbed and murdered is no excuse for infringing on your time and civil rights.

It was a sad state of affairs.

And it was one of the reasons Jack Dakota hadn't gone into police work, though he'd toyed with the idea during his early twenties. Justice meant something to him, always had. But he didn't see much justice in rules and regulations.

Which was why, at thirty, Jack Dakota was a bounty hunter.

You still hunted down the bad guys, but you worked your own hours and got paid for a job and didn't answer to a lot of bureaucratic garbage.

There were still rules, but a smart man knew how to work around them. Jack had always been smart.

He had the papers on his current quarry in his pocket. Ralph Finkleman had called him at eight that morning with the tag. Now, Ralph was a worrier and an optimist—a combination, Jack thought, that must be a job requirement for a bail bondsman. Personally, Jack could never understand the concept of lending money to complete strangers—strangers who, since they needed bond, had already proved themselves unreliable.

But there was money in it, and money was enough motivation for most anything, he supposed.

Jack had just come back from tracing a skip to North Carolina, and had made Ralph pitifully grateful when he hauled in the dumb-as-a-post country boy who'd tried to make his fortune robbing convenience stores. Ralph had put up the bond—claimed he'd figured the kid was too stupid to run.

Jack could have told him, straight off, that the kid was too stupid *not* to run.

But he wasn't being paid to offer advice.

Jack had planned to relax for a few days, maybe take in a few games at Camden Yards, pick one of his female acquaintances to help him enjoy spending his fee. He'd nearly turned Ralph down, but the guy had been so whiny, so full of pleas, he didn't have the heart.

So he'd gone into First Stop Bail Bonds and picked up the paperwork on one M. J. O'Leary, who'd apparently decided against having her day in court to explain why she shot her married boyfriend.

Jack figured she was dumb as a post, as well. A good-looking woman—and from her photo and description, she qualified—with a few working brain cells could manipulate a judge and jury over something as minor as plugging an adulterous accountant.

It wasn't like she'd killed the poor bastard.

It was a cream-puff job, which didn't explain why Ralph had been so jumpy. He'd stuttered more than usual, and his eyes had danced all over the cramped, dusty office.

But Jack wasn't interested in analyzing Ralph. He wanted to wrap up the job quickly, get that beer and start enjoying his fee.

The extra money from this quick one meant he

could snatch up that first edition of *Don Quixote* he'd been coveting, so he'd tolerate sweating in the car for a few hours.

He didn't look like a man who hunted up rare books or enjoyed philosophical debates on the nature of man. He wore his sun-streaked brown hair pulled back in a stubby ponytail—which was more a testament to his distrust of barbers than a fashion statement, though the sleek look enhanced his long, narrow face, with its slashing cheekbones and hollows. Over the shallow dent in his chin, his mouth was full and firm, and looked poetic when it wasn't curled in a sneer.

His eyes were razor-edged gray that could soften to smoke at the sight of the yellowing pages of a first-edition Dante, or darken with pleasure at a glimpse of a pretty woman in a thin summer dress. His brows were arched, with a faintly demonic touch accented by the white scar that ran diagonally through the left and was the result of a tangle with a jackknife wielded by a murder in the second who hadn't wanted Jack to collect his fee.

Jack had collected the fee, and the skip had sported a broken arm and a nose that would never be the same unless the state sprang for rhinoplasty.

Which wouldn't have surprised Jack a bit.

There were other scars. His long, rangy body had the marks of a warrior, and there were women who liked to coo over them.

Jack didn't mind.

He stretched out his yard-long legs, cracked the

tightness out of his shoulders and debated popping the top on another soft drink and pretending it was a beer.

When the MG zipped by, top down, radio blasting, he shook his head. Dumb as a post, he thought—though he admired her taste in music. The car jibed with his paperwork, and the quick glimpse of the woman as she'd flown by confirmed it. The short red hair that had been blowing in the breeze was a dead giveaway.

It was ironic, he thought as he watched her unfold herself out of the little car she'd parked in front of him, that a woman who looked like that should be so pathetically stupid.

He wouldn't have called her easy on the eyes. There didn't look to be anything easy about her. She was a tall one—and he did have a weakness for long-legged, dangerous women. Her narrow teenage-boy hips were hugged by a pair of faded jeans that were white at the stress points and ripped at the knee. The T-shirt tucked into the jeans was plain white cotton, and her small, unhampered breasts pressed nicely against the soft fabric.

She hauled a bag out of the car, and Jack received a interesting view of a firm female bottom in tight denim. Grinning to himself, he patted a hand on his heart. Small wonder some slob had cheated on his wife for this one.

She had a face as angular as her body. Though it was milkmaid-pale, to go with the flaming cap of hair, there was nothing of the maid about it. Pointed chin and pointed cheekbones combined to create a tough, sexy face tilted off center by a lush, sensual mouth.

She was wearing dark wraparound shades, but he knew her eyes were green from the paperwork. He wondered if they'd be like moss or emeralds.

With an enormous shoulder bag hitched on one shoulder, a grocery bag cocked on her hip, she started toward him and the apartment building. He let himself sigh once over her loose-limbed, ground-eating stride.

He sure did go for leggy women.

He got out of the car and strolled after her. He didn't figure she'd be much trouble. She might scratch and bite a bit, but she didn't look like the kind who'd dissolve into pleading tears.

He really hated when that happened.

His game plan was simple. He could have taken her outside, but he hated public displays when there were other choices. So he'd push himself into her apartment, explain the situation, then take her in.

She didn't look like she had a care in the world, Jack noted as he stepped into the building behind her. Did she really figure the cops wouldn't check out the homes of her friends and associates? And driving her own car to shop for groceries. It was amazing she hadn't already been picked up.

But then, the cops had enough to do without scrambling after a woman who'd had a spat with her lover.

He hoped her pal who lived in the apartment

wasn't home. He'd kept the windows under surveillance for the best part of an hour, and he'd seen no movement. He'd heard no sound when he took a lazy walk under the open third-floor windows, and he'd wandered inside to listen at the door.

But you could never be too sure.

Since she turned away from the elevator, toward the stairs, so did he. She never glanced back, making him figure she was either supremely confident or had a lot on her mind.

He closed the distance between them, flashed a smile at her. "Want a hand with that?"

The dark glasses turned, leveled on his face. Her lips didn't curve in the slightest. "No. I've got it."

"Okay, but I'm going a couple flights up. Visiting my aunt. Haven't seen her in—damn—two years. Just blew into town this morning. Forgot how hot it got in D.C."

The glasses turned away again. "It's not the heat," she said, her voice dry as dust, "it's the humidity."

He chuckled at that, recognizing sarcasm and annoyance. "Yeah, that's what they say. I've been in Wisconsin the past few years. Grew up here, though, but I'd forgotten... Here let me give you a hand."

It was a smooth move, easing in as she shifted the bag to slip her key into the lock of the apartment door. Equally smooth, she blocked with her shoulder, pushed the door open. "I've got it," she repeated, and started to kick the door shut in his face.

He slid in like a snake, took a firm hold on her

arm. "Ms. O'Leary—" It was all he got out before her elbow cracked into his chin. He swore, blinked his vision clear and dodged the kick to the groin. But it had been close enough to have him swiftly changing his approach.

Explanations could damn well wait.

He grabbed her, and she turned in his arms, stomped down hard enough on his foot to have stars springing into his head. And that was before she backfisted him in the face.

Her bag of groceries had gone flying, and she delivered each blow with a quick expulsion of breath. Initially he blocked her blows, which wasn't an easy matter. She was obvious trained for combat—a little detail Ralph had omitted.

When she went into a fighting crouch, so did he.

"This isn't going to do you any good." He hated thinking he was going to have to deck her—maybe on that sexy pointed chin. "I'm going to take you in, and I'd rather do it without messing you up."

Her answer was a swift flying kick to his midsection he wished he'd been able to admire from a distance. But he was too busy crashing into a table.

Damn, she was good.

He expected her to bolt for the door, and was up on the balls of his feet quickly to block her. But she merely circled him, eyes hidden behind the dark glasses, mouth curled in a grimace.

"Come on, then," she taunted him. "Nobody tries to mug me on my own turf and walks away."

"I'm not a mugger." He kicked away a trio of

firm, ripe peaches that had spilled out of her bag. "I'm a skip tracer, and you're busted." He held up a hand, signaling peace, and, hoping her gaze had flickered there, moved in fast, hooked a foot under her leg and sent her sprawling on her butt.

He tackled her, and might have appreciated the long, economical lines of her body pressed beneath him, but her knee had better aim than her initial kick. His eyes rolled, his breath hissed, as the pain only a man understands radiated in sick waves. But he hung on.

He had the advantage now, and she knew it. Vertical, she was fast, and her reach was nearly as long as his and the odds were more balanced. But in a wrestling match, he outweighed her and outmuscled her. It infuriated her enough to have her resorting to dirty tactics. She fixed her teeth in his shoulders like a bear trap, felt the adrenaline and satisfaction rush through her as he howled.

They rolled, limbs tangling, hands grappling, and crashed into the coffee table. A wide blue bowl filled with chocolate drops shattered on the floor. A shard pierced his undamaged shoulder and made him swear again. She landed a blow to the side of his head, another to his kidneys.

She was just beginning to think she could take him, after all, when he flipped her over. She landed with a jarring smack, and before she could suck in breath, he had her hands locked behind her back and was sitting on her.

The fact that his breath was coming in pants was

very little satisfaction. And for the first time, she was seriously afraid.

"Don't know why the hell you shot the guy, when you could've just beat the hell out of him," Jack muttered. He reached into his back pocket for his cuffs, swore again when he came up empty. They'd popped out during the match.

He simply rode her out as she bucked, and caught his breath. He hadn't had a fight of this magnitude with a female since he hunted down Big Betsy. And she'd been two hundred pounds of sheer muscle.

"Look, it's only going to be harder on you this way. Why don't you just go quietly, before we bust up any more of your friend's apartment?"

"You're crushing me, you jerk," she said between her teeth. "And this is my apartment. You try to rape me, and I'll twist your pride clean off and hand it to you. There won't be enough left of you for the cops to scrape off their shoes."

"I don't force women, sugar. Just because some accountant couldn't keep his hands off you doesn't mean I can't. And the cops aren't interested in me. They want you."

She blew out a breath, tried to suck another in, but he was crushing her lungs. "I don't know what the hell you're talking about."

He pulled the papers out of his pocket, shoved them in front of her face. "M. J. O'Leary, assault with a deadly, malicious wounding, and blah-blah. Ralph's real disappointed in you, sugar. He's a trusting man and didn't expect a nice woman like you to try to skip out on the ten-K bond.''

"This is a crock." She could see her name and some downtown address on what appeared to be some kind of arrest warrant. "You've got the wrong person. I didn't post bail for anything. I haven't been arrested, and I live here. Idiot cops," she muttered, and tried to buck him off again. "Call in to your sergeant, or whatever. Straighten this out. And when you do, I'm suing."

"Nice try. And I suppose you've never heard of George MacDonald."

"No, I haven't."

"Then it was really rude of you to shoot him." He eased up just enough to flip her face up, then caught both of her hands at the wrist. She'd lost her glasses, he noted, and her eyes were neither moss nor emerald, he decided—they were dark shady-river green. And, just now, full of fury. "Look, you want to have a hot affair with your accountant, sister, it's no skin off my nose. You want to shoot him, I don't particularly care. But you skip bond, and it ticks me off."

She could breathe slightly easier now, but his hands were like steel bands at her wrists. "My accountant's name is Holly Bergman, and we haven't had a hot affair. I haven't shot anyone, and I haven't *skipped* bond because I haven't *posted* bond. I want to see your ID, ace."

He thought it took a lot of nerve to make demands

in her current position. "My name's Dakota, Jack Dakota. I'm a skip tracer."

Her eyes narrowed as they skimmed over his face. She thought he looked like something out of the gritty side of a western. A cold-eyed gunslinger, a tough-talking gambler. Or...

"A bounty hunter. Well, there's no bounty here, jerk." It wasn't rape, and it wasn't a mugging. The fear that had iced her heart thawed into fresh temper. "You son of a bitch. You break in here, tear up my things, ruin twenty bucks' worth of produce, and all because you can't follow the right trail? Your butt's in a sling, I promise you. When I'm done, you won't be able to trace your own name with a stencil. You won't—" She broke off when he stuck a photo in her face.

It was her face, and the photograph might have been taken yesterday.

"Got a twin, O'Leary? One who drives a '68 MG, license plate SLAINTE, and is currently shacked up with some guy named Bailey James."

"Bailey's a woman," she murmured, staring at her own face while new worries raced in her head. Was this about Bailey, about what Bailey had sent her? What kind of trouble could her friend be in? "And this isn't her apartment, it's mine. I don't have a twin." She looked up into his eyes again. "What's going on? Is Bailey all right? Where's Bailey?"

Under his clamped hands, her pulse had spiked. She was struggling again, with a fresh and vicious energy he knew was brought on by fear. And he was dead certain it wasn't fear for herself.

"I don't know anything about this Bailey except this address is listed under her name on the paperwork."

But he was beginning to smell something, and he didn't like it. He was no longer thinking M. J. O'Leary was dumb as a post. A woman with any brains wouldn't have left herself with so many avenues to be tracked if she was on the run.

Ralph, Jack mused, frowning down into M.J.'s face. Why were you so jumpy this morning?

"If you're being straight with me, we can confirm it quick enough. Maybe it was a clerical mix-up." But he didn't think so. No indeed. And there was an itching at the base of his spine. "Listen," he began, just as the door broke open and the giant roared in.

"You were supposed to bring her out," the giant said, and waved an impressive .357 Magnum. "You're talking too much. He's waiting."

Jack didn't have much time to decide how to play it. The big man was a stranger to him, but he recognized the type. It looked like all bulk and no brains, with the huge bullet head, small eyes and massive shoulders. The gun was big as a cannon and looked like a toy in the ham-size hands.

"Sorry." He gave M.J.'s wrist a quick squeeze, hoping she'd understand it as a sign of reassurance and remain still and quiet. "I was having a little trouble here."

"Just a woman. You were supposed to just bring the woman out."

"Yeah, I was working on it." Jack tried a friendly smile. "Ralph send you to back me up?"

"Come on, up. Up now. We're going."

"Sure. No problem. You won't need the gun now. I've got her under control." But the gun continued to point, its barrel as wide as Montana, at his head.

"Just her." And the giant smiled, floppy lips peeling back over huge teeth. "We don't need you now."

"Fine. I guess you want the paperwork." For lack of anything better, Jack snagged a can of tomato sauce on his way up and winged it. It made a satisfactory crunching sound on the big man's nose. Ducking, Jack rushed forward like a battering ram. It felt a great deal like beating his head against a brick wall, but the force took them both tumbling backward and over a ladder-back chair.

The gun went off, putting a fist-size hole in the ceiling before it flew across the room.

She thought about running. She could have been out of the door and away before either of them untangled. But she thought about Bailey, about what she had weighing down her shoulder bag. About the mess she'd somehow stepped in. And was too mad to run.

She went for the gun and ended up falling backward as Jack flew into her. She cushioned his fall, and he was up fast, springing into the air and landing a double-footed kick in the big man's midsection.

Nice form, M.J. thought, and scrambled to her own feet. She snagged her shoulder bag, spun it over her head and cracked it hard over the sleek, bullet-shaped head.

He went down hard on the sofa, snapping the springs.

"You're wrecking my place!" she shouted, and smacked Jack in the side, simply because she could reach him.

"Sue me."

He dodged a fist the size of a steamship and went in low. Pain sang through every bone as his opponent slammed him into a wall. Pictures fell, glass shattering on the floor. Through his blurred vision he saw the woman charge, a redheaded fireball that flew up and latched like a plague of wasps on the man's enormous back. She used her fists, pounding the sides of his face as he spun wildly and struggled to grab her.

"Hold him still!" Jack shouted. "Damn it, just hold him for a minute!"

Spotting an opening, he grabbed what was left of a table leg and rushed in. He checked his first swing as the duo spun like a mad two-headed top. If he followed through, he might have cracked the back of M.J.'s head open like a melon.

"I said hold him still!"

"You want me to paint a bull's-eye on his face while I'm at it?" With a guttural snarl, she hooked her arms around the man's throat, clamped her thighs like a vise around his wide steel beam of a torso and screamed, "Hit him, for God's sake. Stop dancing around and hit him."

Jack cocked back like a batter with two strikes already on his record and swung full out. The table leg splintered like a toothpick, blood gushed like water in a fountain. M.J. had just enough time to jump clear as the man toppled like a redwood.

She stayed on her hands and knees a minute, gasping for air. "What's going on? What the hell's going on?"

"No time to worry about it." Self-preservation on his mind, Jack grabbed her hand, hauled her to her feet. "This type doesn't usually travel alone. Let's go."

"Go?" She snagged the strap of her purse as he pulled her toward the door. "Where?"

"Away. He's going to be mean when he wakes up, and if he's got a friend, we're not going to be so lucky next time."

"Lucky, my butt." But she was running with him, driven by a pure instinct that matched Jack's. "You son of a bitch. You come busting into my place, push me around, wreck my home, nearly get me shot."

"I saved your butt."

"I saved *yours!*" She shouted it at him, cursing viciously as they thudded down the stairs. "And when I get a minute to catch my breath, I'm going to take you apart, piece by piece."

They rounded the landing and nearly ran over one of her neighbors. The woman, with helmet hair and bunny slippers, cowered, back against the wall, hands pressed to her deeply rouged cheeks.

"M.J., what in the world—? Were those gunshots?"

"Mrs. Weathers—"

"No time." Jack all but jerked her off her feet as he headed down the next flight.

"Don't you shout at me, you jerk. I'm making you pay for every grape that got smashed, every lamp, every—"

"Yeah, yeah, I get the picture. Where's the back door?" When M.J. pointed down the corridor, he gave a nod and they both slid outside, then around the corner of the building. Screened by some bushes in the front, Jack darted a gaze up and down the street. There was a windowless van less than half a block down, and a small, chicken-faced man in a bad suit dancing beside it. "Stay low," Jack ordered, thankful he'd parked right out front as they ran down the walkway and he all but threw M.J. into the front seat of his car.

"My God, what the hell is this?" She shoved at the can she'd sat on, kicked at the wrappers littering the floor, then joined them when Jack put a hand behind her head and shoved.

"Low!" he repeated in a snarl, and gunned the engine. The faint ping told him the man with the chicken face was using the silenced automatic he'd pulled out.

Jack's car screamed away from the curb, and he two-wheeled it around the corner and shot down the street like a rocket. Tossed like eggs in a broken carton, M.J. rapped her head on the dash, cursed, and struggled to balance herself as Jack maneuvered the huge boat of a car down side streets.

"What the hell are you doing?"

"Saving your butt again, sugar." His eyes flicked to the rearview as he took a hard, tire-squealing right turn. A couple of kids riding bikes on the sidewalk lifted their fists and cheered the maneuver. In instant reaction, Jack flashed a grin.

"Slow this junk heap down." M.J. had to crawl back onto the seat and clutch the chicken stick for balance. "And let me out before you run over some kid walking his dog."

"I'm not going to run over anybody, and you're staying put." He spared her a quick glance. "In case you didn't notice, the guy with the van was shooting at us. And as soon as I make sure we've lost him and find someplace quiet to hole up, you're going to tell me what the hell's going on."

"I don't know what's going on."

He shot her a look. "That's bull."

Because he was sure it was, he took a chance. He swung to the curb again, reached under his seat and came up with spare cuffs. Before she could do more than blink, he had her locked by the wrist to the door handle. No way was she skipping out on him until he knew why he'd just been tossed around by a three-hundred-pound gorilla.

To block out her shouting, and her increasingly imaginative threats and curses, Jack turned up his stereo and drowned her out.

Chapter 2

At the very first opportunity, she was going to kill him. Brutally, M.J. decided. Mercilessly. Two hours before this, she'd been happy, free, wandering around the grocery store like any normal person on a Saturday, squeezing tomatoes. True, she'd been weighed down with curiosity about what she carried in the bottom of her purse, but she'd been sure Bailey had a good reason—and a logical explanation—for sending it to her.

Bailey James always had good reasons and logical explanations for everything. That was only one of the aspects about her that M.J. loved.

But now she was worried—worried that the package Bailey had shipped to her by courier the day before was not only at the bottom of her purse, but also at the bottom of her current situation.

She preferred blaming Jack Dakota.

He'd pushed his way into her apartment and attacked her. Okay, so maybe she'd attacked first, but it was a natural reaction when some jerk tried to muscle you. At least it was M.J.'s natural reaction. She was an ace student in the school of punch first, ask questions later.

It was humiliating that he'd been able to take her down. She had a lot of notches on her fifth-degree black belt, and she didn't like to lose a match.

But she'd pay him back for that later.

All she knew for certain was that he seemed to be at the root of it all. Because of him, her apartment was wrecked, her things tossed every which way. Now they'd gone, leaving the front door open, the lock broken. She didn't form close attachments to things, but that wasn't the point. They were *her* things, and thanks to him, she was going to have to waste time shopping for replacements.

Which was almost as bad as having some gun-wielding punk the size of Texas busting down her door, having to run for her life from her own home, and being shot at.

But all of that, all of it, paled next to one infuriating fact—she was handcuffed to the door handle of an Oldsmobile.

Jack Dakota had to die for that.

Who the hell was he? she asked herself. Bounty hunter, excellent hand-to-hand fighter, slob—she added as she pushed candy wrappers and paper cups around with her foot—and nerveless driver. Under different circumstances, she'd have been impressed by the way he handled the tank of a car, swinging it around curves, screaming around corners, whipping it through yellow lights and zipping onto the Washington Beltway like the leader in a Grand Prix event.

If he'd walked into her bar, she'd have looked twice, she admitted grudgingly. Running a pub in a major city meant more than being able to mix drinks and work the books. It meant being able to size people up quickly, tell the troublemakers from the lonely hearts. And know how to deal with both.

She'd have tagged him as a tough customer. It was in his face. A damn good face, all in all, hard and handsome. Yeah, she'd have looked twice, M.J. thought, teeth gritted, as she looked out the window of the speeding car. Pretty boys didn't interest her much. She preferred a man who looked as though he'd lived, crossed a few lines and would cross a few more.

Jack Dakota fit that bill. She'd gotten a good close look into those eyes—granite gray—and knew that he wasn't one to let a few rules get in his way.

Just what would a man like him do if he knew she was carrying a king's ransom in her battered leather purse?

Damn it, Bailey. Damn it. M.J. fisted her free hand and tapped it restlessly on her knee. Why did you send me the diamond, and where are the other two?

She cursed herself, as well, for not going directly to Bailey's door after she came home from closing M.J.'s the night before. But she'd been tired, and she'd figured Bailey was sound asleep. And as her friend was the steadiest, most practical person M.J. knew, she'd simply decided to wait for what she was certain would be a very practical, sensible reason.

Stupid, she told herself now. Why had she assumed Bailey had sent the stone to her simply because she knew M.J. would be home in the middle of the day and around to receive the package? Why had she assumed the rock was a fake, a copy, even though the note that accompanied it asked M.J. to keep it with her at all times?

Because Bailey just wasn't the kind of woman to ship off a blue diamond worth more than a million with no warnings or explanations. She was a gemologist, dedicated, brilliant, and patient as Job. How else could she continue to work for the creeps who masqueraded as her family?

M.J.'s mouth tightened as she thought of Bailey's stepbrothers. The Salvini twins had always treated Bailey as though she were an inconvenience, something they were stuck with because their father had left her a percentage of the business in his will. And, blindly loyal to family, Bailey had always found excuses for them.

Now M.J. wondered if they were part of the reason. Had they tried to pull something? She wouldn't put it past them, no indeed. But it was hard to believe Timothy and Thomas Salvini would be stupid enough to try something fancy with the Three Stars of Mithra.

That was what Bailey had called them, and she'd

had a dreamy look in her eyes. Three priceless blue diamonds, in a golden triangle that had once been held in the open hands of a statue of the god Mithra, and now property of the Smithsonian. Salvini, with Bailey's reputation behind it, was to assess, verify and appraise the stones.

What if the creeps had gotten it into their heads to keep them?

No, it was too wild, M.J. decided. Better to believe this whole mess was some sort of mix-up, a mistaken identity tangle.

Much better to concentrate on how she would re-pay Jack Dakota for ruining her afternoon off.

"You are a dead man." She said it calmly, relishing the words.

"Yeah, well, everybody dies sooner or later." He was heading south on 95, and he was grateful she'd stopped swearing at him long enough to let him think.

"It's going to be sooner in your case, Jack. Lots sooner." The traffic was thick, thanks to the Fourth of July holiday weekend, but it was fast.

How humiliating would it be, she wondered, to stick her head out the window and scream for help? Mortifying, she supposed, but she might have tried it if she'd believed it would work. Better if they could just run into one of the inexplicable traffic snags that stopped cars dead for miles.

Where the hell were the road crews and the rub-berneckers who loved them when she needed them?

Seeing nothing but clear sailing for miles, she told

herself to deal with Jack "The Idiot" Dakota herself. "If you want to live to see another sunrise, pull this excuse for a car over, uncuff me and let me go."

"Go where?" He flicked his eyes from the road long enough to glance at her. "Back to your apartment?"

"That's my problem, not yours."

"Not anymore, sister. I take it personal, real personal, when someone shoots at me. Since you seem to be the reason why, I'll be keeping you for a while."

If they hadn't been doing seventy, she'd have punched him. Instead, she rattled her chain. "Take these damn things off me."

"Nope."

A muscle twitched in her jaw. "You've stepped in it now, Dakota. We're in Virginia. Kidnapping, crossing state lines. That's federal."

"You came with me," he pointed out. "Now you're staying with me until I get this figured out." The doors rattled ominously as he whipped around an eighteen-wheeler. "And you should be grateful."

"Oh, I should be grateful. You broke into my apartment, knocked me around, busted up my things and have me cuffed to a door handle."

"That's right. If I hadn't, you'd probably be lying in that apartment right now, with a bullet in your head."

"They came after you, ace, not me."

"I don't think so. My debts are paid, I'm not fooling around with anyone's wife, and I haven't pissed anyone off lately. Except for you. Nobody's got a reason to send muscle after me. You, on the other hand…'' He skimmed his gaze over her face again. ''Somebody wants you, sugar.''

''Thousands do,'' she said, stretched out her long legs as she shifted toward him.

''I'll bet.'' He didn't give in to the impulse to look at those legs—he just thought about them. ''But other than the brainless idiots you'd kick in the heart, you've got someone real interested. Interested enough to set me up, and take me out with you. Ralph, you bastard.''

He shoved aside a copy of *The Grapes of Wrath* and a torn T-shirt and snagged his car phone. Steering one-handed, he punched in numbers then hooked the receiver under his chin.

''Ralph, you bastard,'' he repeated when the phone was answered.

''D-D-Dakota? That you? You track d-d-down that skip?''

''When I figure my way clear of this, I'm coming for you.''

''What—what're you talking about? You find her? Look, it's a straight trace, Jack. I g-g-gave you a plum. Just a c-c-couple's hours' work for full f-f-fee.''

''You're stuttering more than usual, Ralph. That won't be a problem after I knock your teeth down your throat. Who wants the woman?''

''Look, I—I—I got problems here. I gotta close

early. It's the holiday weekend. I got p-p-personal problems."

"There's no place you can hide. Why the phony paperwork? Why'd you set me up?"

"I got p-p-problems. Big p-p-problems."

"I'm your big problem right now." He tapped the brakes, swung around a convertible and hit the fast lane. "If whoever's pushing your buttons is trying to trace this, I'm in my car, just tooling around." He thought for a moment, then added, "And I've got the woman."

"Jack, listen to me. L-l-listen. Tell me where you are, dump her and d-d-drive away. J-j-just drive. Stay out of it. I wouldn'ta tagged you for the job, 'cept I knew you could handle yourself. Now I'm telling you, stash her somewhere, give me the l-l-location and drive away. Far away. You don't want this."

"Who wants her, Ralph?"

"You don't n-n-need to know. You d-d-don't want to know. Just d-d-do it. I'll throw in five large. A b-b-bonus."

"Five large?" Jack's brows lifted. When Ralph parted with an extra nickel, it was big. "Make it ten and tell me who wants her, and we may deal."

It pleased him that M.J. protested that with a flurry of curses and threats. It added substance to the bluff.

"T-t-ten!" Ralph squeaked it, stuttered for a full ten seconds. "Okay, okay, ten grand, but no names, and b-b-believe me, Jack, I'm saving your life here. Just t-t-tell me where you're going to stash her."

Smiling grimly, Jack made a pithy and anatomically impossible suggestion, then disconnected.

"Well, sugar, your hide's now worth ten thousand to me. We're going to find a nice, quiet spot so you can tell me why I shouldn't collect."

He zipped off an exit, did a quick turnaround and headed back north.

Her mouth was dry. She wanted to believe it was from shouting, but there was fear clawing at her throat. "Where are you going?"

"Just covering my tracks. They wouldn't get much of a trace on a cellular, but it doesn't hurt to be cautious."

"You're taking me back?"

He didn't look at her, and didn't grin. Though the waver of nerves in her voice pleased him. If she was scared enough, she'd talk. "Ten thousand's a hefty incentive, sugar. Let's see if you can convince me you're worth more alive."

He knew just what he was looking for. He trolled the secondary roads, skimming through the holiday traffic. He'd forgotten it was the Fourth of July weekend. Which was just as well, he thought, as it didn't look like there were going to be a lot of opportunities to kick back with that cold beer and watch any fireworks.

Unless they came from the woman beside him.

She was a firecracker, all right. She had to be afraid by now, but she was holding her own. He was grateful for that. There was nothing more irritating than a whiner. But scared or not, he was certain she'd try to take a chunk out of him at the first opportunity.

He didn't intend to give her one.

With any luck, once they were settled, he'd have the full story out of her within a couple hours.

Then maybe he'd help her out of her jam. For a fee, that is. It could be a small one because at this point he was ticked and figured he had a vested interest in dealing with whoever had set him on her.

Whoever it was, they'd gone to a great deal of trouble. But they hadn't picked their goons very well. He could figure the scam well enough. Once he captured his quarry and had her secured and in his car, the men in the van would have run them off the road. He'd have figured it to be the action of a competing bounty hunter, and though he wouldn't have given up his fee without a fight, he'd have been outnumbered and outgunned.

Skip tracers didn't go crying to the cops when a competitor snatched their bounty.

The goons might have let him off with a few bruises, maybe a minor concussion. But the way that mountain of a man had been waving his cannon in M.J.'s apartment, Jack thought it was far more likely that he'd have sported a brand-new hole in some vital part of his body.

Because the mountain had been an moron.

So at this point he was on the run with an angry woman, a little over three hundred in cash and a quarter tank of gas.

He intended to know why.

He spotted what he was after north of Leesburg, Virginia. The tourists and holiday travelers, unless they were very down on their luck, would give a dilapidated dump like the Kountry Klub Motel a wide berth. But the low-slung building with the paint peeling on the green doors and the pitted parking lot met Jack's requirements perfectly.

He pulled to the farthest end of the lot, away from the huddle of rusted cars near the check-in, and cut the engine.

"Is this where you bring all your dates, Dakota?"

He smiled at her, a quick flash of teeth that was unexpectedly charming. "Only first class for you, sugar."

He knew just what she was thinking. The minute he cut her loose, she'd be all over him like spandex. And if she could get out of the car, she'd be sprinting toward the check-in as fast as those mile-long legs would carry her.

"I don't expect you to believe me." He said it casually as he leaned over to unlock the cuff from the door handle. "But I'm not going to enjoy this."

She was braced. He could feel her body tense to spring. He had to be quick, and he had to be rough. She'd no more than hissed out a breath before he had her hands secured and locked behind her. She sucked in air just as he clamped a hand over her mouth.

She bucked and rolled, tried to bring up her legs to kick, but he pinned her on the seat, flipped her facedown. He was out of breath by the time he'd tied the bandanna over her mouth.

"I lied." Panting, he rubbed the fresh bruise where her elbow had connected with his ribs. "Maybe I enjoyed that a little."

He used the torn T-shirt to tie her legs, tried not to appreciate overmuch the length and shape of them. But, hell, he was only human. Once he had her trussed up like a turkey, he looped the slack of the handcuffs around the gearshift, then wound up the windows.

"Hot as hell, isn't it?" he said conversationally. "Well, I won't be long." He locked the car and walked away whistling.

It took her a moment to regain her balance. She was scared, she realized. Really, bone-deep scared, and she couldn't remember if she'd ever felt this kind of mind-numbing panic before. She was trembling, and had to stop. It wouldn't help her out of this fix.

Once, when she'd just opened her pub, she'd been closing down late at night. She'd been alone when the man came in and demanded money. She'd been scared then, too, terrified by the wild look in his eyes that shouted drugs. So she'd handed over the till, just as the cops recommended.

Then she'd handed him the fat end of the Louisville Slugger she had behind the bar.

She'd been scared, but she'd dealt with it.

She would deal with this, too.

The gag tasted of man and infuriated her. She couldn't push or wiggle or slide it out, so she gave up on it and concentrated on freeing the loop of the cuffs. If she could free her hands from the gearshift,

she could fold herself up, bend her legs through her
arms and get some mobility.

She was agile, she told herself. She was strong and
she was smart. Oh, God, she was scared. She moaned
and whimpered in frustration. The handcuffs might
as well have been cemented to the gearshift.

If she could only see, twist herself around so that
she could see what she was doing. She struggled, all
but dislocating her shoulder, until she managed to
flip around. Sweat seemed to boil over her, dripped
into her eyes as she yanked at the steel.

She stopped herself, closed her eyes and got her
breath back. She used her shaking fingers to probe,
to trace along the steel, slide over the smooth length
of the gearshift. Keeping them closed, she visualized
what she was doing, carefully, slowly, shifting her
hands until she felt steel begin to slide. Her shoulders
screamed as she forced them into an unnatural position, but she bit down on the gag and twisted.

She felt something give, hoped it wasn't a joint,
then collapsed in an exhausted, sweaty heap as the
cuffs slipped off the stick.

"Damn, you're good," Jack commented as he
wrenched open the door. He dragged her out and
tossed her over his shoulder. "Another five minutes,
you might have pulled it off." He carried her into a
room at the end of the concrete block. He'd already
unlocked the door, and he'd paused for a minute to
observe, and admire, her struggles before he came
back to the car.

Now he dumped her on the bed. Because her

adrenaline was back and she was fighting him, he simply lay flat on her back, letting her bounce until she was worn out.

And he enjoyed that, too. He wasn't proud of it, he thought, but he enjoyed it. The woman had incredible energy and staying power. If they'd met under different circumstances, he imagined they could have torn up those cheap motel sheets like maniacs and parted as friends.

As it was, he was going to have a hard time not imagining her naked.

Maybe he lay on her, smelled her, just a little longer than necessary. He wasn't a saint, was he? he asked himself grimly as he unlocked one of her hands and secured the cuff to the iron headboard.

He rose, ran a hand through his hair. "You're making this tougher than necessary for both of us," he told her, as she murdered him with a scalding look out of hot green eyes. He was out of breath and knew he couldn't blame it entirely on the last, minor skirmish. That tight little bottom of hers pressing against his crotch had left him uncomfortably aroused.

And he didn't want to be.

Turning from her, he switched on the TV, let the volume boom out. M.J. had already ripped the gag away with her free hand and was hissing like a snake. "You can scream all you want now," he told her as he took out a small knife and sliced through the phone cord. "The three rooms down from here are vacant, so nobody's going to hear you." Then he grinned. "Besides, I put it around at check-in that we're on our honeymoon, so even if they hear, they're not going to bother us. Be back in a minute.''

He went out, shutting the door behind him.

M.J. closed her eyes again. Dear God, what was going on with her? For a moment, for just one insane moment, when he pressed her into the mattress with his body, she'd felt weak and hot. With lust.

It was sick, sick, sick.

But just for that one insane moment, she'd imagined being stripped and taken, being ravaged, having his mouth on her. His hands on her.

More, she'd wanted it.

She shuddered now, praying it was just some sort of weird reaction to shock.

She wasn't a woman who shied away from good, healthy, hot sex. But she didn't give herself to strangers, to men who knocked her down, tied her up and tossed her into bed in some cheap motel.

And he'd been aroused. She hadn't been so stupid, or so dazed with shock, that she was unaware of his reaction. Hell, the man had been wrapped around her, hadn't he? But he'd backed off.

She struggled to even her breathing. He wasn't going to rape her. He didn't want sex. He wanted— God only knew.

Don't feel, she ordered herself. Just think. Just clear your mind and think.

Slowly, she opened her eyes, took a survey of the room.

It was, in a word, hideous.

Obviously, some misguided soul had thought that

using an eye-searing combo of orange and blue would turn the cheaply furnished, cramped little room into the exotic.

He couldn't have been more wrong.

The drapes were as thin as paper, and looked to be of about the same consistency. But he'd pulled them closed over the narrow front window, so the room was deep in shadow.

The television blared out a poorly dubbed Hercules movie on its rickety gray pedestal. The single dresser was ringed with interlinking watermarks. There was a metal box beside the bed. For a couple of bucks in quarters, she could treat herself to dancing fingers. Whoopee.

The yellow glass ashtray on the night table was chipped, and didn't look heavy enough to make an effective weapon. Even over the din of Hercules, she could hear the roaring sputter of an air-conditioning unit that was doing absolutely nothing to cool the room.

The print near a narrow door she assumed was to the bathroom was a garish reproduction of a country landscape in autumn, complete with screaming red barn and stupid-faced cows.

Reaching over, she tested the bedside lamp. It was bright blue glass, with a dingy and yellowing shade, but it had some heft. It might come in handy.

She heard the rattle of the key and set it down again, stared at the door.

He came in with a small red-and-white cooler and dropped it on the dresser. Her heart thumped when she saw her purse slung over his shoulder, but he tossed it on the floor by the bed so casually that she relaxed again.

The diamond was still safe, she thought. And so was the can of Mace, the can opener and the roll of nickels she habitually carried as weapons.

"Nothing I like better than a really bad movie," he commented, and paused to watch Hercules battle several fierce-looking warriors sporting pelts and bad teeth. "I always wonder where they come up with the dialogue. You know, was it really that bad when it was scripted in Lithuanian or whatever, or does it just lose it in the translation?"

With a shrug, he walked over, lifted the top on the cooler and took out two soft drinks.

"I figure you're thirsty." He walked to her, offered a can. "And you're not the type to cut off your nose." His assessment was proved correct when she grabbed the can and drank deeply. "This place doesn't run to room service," he continued. "But there's a diner down the road, so we won't go hungry. You want something now?"

She eyed him over the top of the can. "No."

"Fine." He sat on the side of the bed, settled himself and smiled at her. "Let's talk."

"Kiss my butt."

He blew out a breath. "It's an attractive offer, sugar, but I've been trying not to think along those lines." He gave her thigh a friendly pat. "Now, the way I see it, we're both in a jam here, and you've got the key. Once you tell me who's after you and why, I'll deal with it."

The worst of her thirst was abated, so she sipped slowly. Her voice dripped sarcasm. "*You'll* deal with it?"

"Yeah. Consider me your champion-at-arms. Like good old Herc there." He stabbed a thumb at the set behind him. "You tell me about it, then I'll go take care of the bad guys. Then I'll bill you. And if the offer about kissing your butt's still open, I'll take you up on that, too."

"Let's see." She leaned her head back, kept her eyes level on his. "What was it you told your pal Ralph to do? Oh, yeah." She peeled her lips back in a snarl and repeated it.

He only shook his head. "Is that any way to talk to the guy who kept you from getting a bullet in the brain?"

"*I* kept *you* from getting a bullet in the brain, pal, though I have serious doubts he'd have been able to hit it, as it's clearly so small. And you pay me back by manhandling me, tying me up, gagging me, and dumping me in some cheap rent-by-the-hour motel."

"I'm assured this is a family establishment," he said dryly. God, she was a pistol, he thought. Spitting at him despite his advantage, daring him to take her on, though she didn't have a hope of winning the game. And sexy as bloody hell in tight jeans and a wrinkled shirt.

"Think about this," he said. "That brainless giant said something about me taking too long, talking too much, which leads me to believe they were listening from the van. They must have had surveillance equipment, and he got antsy. Otherwise, if you'd gone along with me like a good girl, they'd have pulled us over somewhere along the line and taken you. They didn't want direct involvement, or witnesses.''

"You'd be a witness," she corrected.

"Nothing to sweat over. I'd have been ticked off about having another bounty hunter snatch my job, but people in my line of work don't go running to the cops. I'd have lost my fee, considered my day wasted, maybe bitched to Ralph. That's the way they'd figure it, anyway. And Ralph would have probably passed me some fluff job to keep me happy.''

His eyes changed, went hard again. Knife-edged gray ice. "Somebody's got their foot on his throat. I want to know who.''

"I couldn't say. I don't know your friend Ralph—''

"Former friend.''

"I don't know the gorilla who broke my door, and I don't know you.'' She was pleased her voice was calm, without a single hitch or quiver. "Now, if you'll let me go, I'll report all this to the police.''

His lips twitched. "That's the first time you've mentioned the cops, sugar. And you're bluffing. You don't want them in on this. That's another question.''

He was right about that. She didn't want the police, not until she'd talked to Bailey and knew what was going on. But she shrugged, glanced toward the phone he'd put out of commission. "You could call my bluff if you hadn't wrecked the phone."

"You wouldn't call the cops, but whoever you called might have their phone tapped. I didn't go through all the trouble to find us these plush out-of-the-way surroundings to get traced."

He leaned over, took her chin in his hand. "Who would you call, M.J.?"

She kept her eyes steady, fighting to ignore the heat of his fingers, the texture of his skin against hers. "My lover." She spit the words out. "He'd take you apart limb by limb. He'd rip out your heart, then show it to you while it was still beating."

He smiled, eased a little closer. He just couldn't resist. "What's his name?"

Her mind was blank, totally, completely, foolishly blank. She stared into those slate-gray eyes a moment, then shook his hand away. "Hank. He'll break you in half and toss you to the dogs when he finds out you've messed with me."

He chuckled, infuriated her. "You may have a lover, sugar. You may have a dozen. But you don't have one named Hank. Took you too long. Okay, you don't want to spill it and rely on me to work us out of this, we'll go another route."

He rose, leaned over. He heard her quickly in-drawn breath when he reached down for her purse. Without a word, he dumped the contents on the bed. He'd already removed the weapons. "You ever use that can opener for more than popping a beer?'' he asked her.

"How dare you! How dare you go through my things!"

"Oh, I think this is small potatoes after what we've been through together.'' He picked up the velvet pouch, slid the stone into his hand, where it flashed like fire, despite its lowly surroundings.

He admired it, as he had been unable to in the car, when he searched her bag. It was deeply, brilliantly blue, big as a baby's fist and cut to shoot blue flame. He felt a tug as it lay nestled in his hand, an odd need to protect it. Almost as inexplicable, he thought, as his odd need to protect this prickly, ungrateful woman.

"So.'' He sat, tossing the stone up, catching it. "Tell me about this, M.J. Just where did you get your hands on a blue diamond big enough to choke a cat?''

Chapter 3

Options whirled through her mind. The simplest, and the most satisfying, she thought, was to make him feel like a fool.

"Are you crazy?" She rolled her eyes and scoffed. "Yeah, that's a diamond, all right, a big blue one. I carry a green one in my glove compartment, and a pretty red one in my other purse. I spend all the profits from my pub on diamonds. It's a weakness."

He studied her, idly tossing the stone, catching it. She looked annoyed, he decided. Amused and cocky. "So what is it?"

"A paperweight, for God's sake."

He waited a beat. "You carry a paperweight in your purse."

Hell. "It was a gift." She said it primly, her nose in the air.

"Yeah, from Hank the Hunk, no doubt." He rose, casually pushed through the rest of the contents he'd dumped out. "Let's see, other than the blackjack—"

"It was a roll of nickels," she corrected.

"Same effect. Mace, a can opener I doubt you cart around to pop Bud bottles, we've got an electronic organizer, a wallet with more photos than cash—"

"I don't appreciate you rifling my personal belongings."

"Sue me. A bottle of designer water, six pens, four pencils. Some eyeliner, matches, keys, two pair of sunglasses, a paperback copy of Sue Grafton's latest—good book, by the way, I won't tell you the ending—a candy bar..." He tossed it to her. "In case you're hungry. A flip phone." He tucked that in his back pocket. "About three dollars in loose change, a weather radio and a box of condoms." He lifted a brow. "Unopened. But then, you never know."

Heat, a combination of mortification and fury, crawled up her neck. "Pervert."

"I'd say you're a woman who believes in being prepared. So why not carry a paperweight around with you? You might run into a stack of paper that needs anchoring. Happens all the time."

He made a couple of swipes to gather and dump the items scattered on the bed back into her bag, then tossed it aside. "I won't ask what kind of fool you take me for, because I've already got that picture." Moving to the mirror over the dresser, he scraped the stone diagonally across the glass. It left a long, thin scratch.

"They just don't make motel mirrors like they used to," he commented, then came back and sat on the bed beside her. "Now, back to my original question. What are you doing with a blue diamond big enough to choke a cat?"

When she said nothing, he vised her chin in his hand, jerked her face to his. "Listen, sister, I could truss you up again, leave you here and walk away with your million-dollar paperweight. That's door number one. I can kick back, watch the movie and wait you out, because sooner or later you'll tell me what I want to know. That's door number two. Behind door number three, you tell me now why you're carrying a stone that could buy a small island in the West Indies and we start figuring out how to get us both out of this jam."

She didn't flinch, she didn't blink. He had to admire the sheer nerve. Because he did, he waited patiently while she studied him out of those deep green cat-tilted eyes.

"Why haven't you taken door number one already?"

"Because I don't like having some gorilla try to break me in half, I don't like getting shot at, and I don't like being hosed by some skinny woman with an attitude." He leaned closer, until they were nose-to-nose. "I've got debts to pay on this one, sugar. And you're the first stop."

She grabbed his wrist with her free hand, shoved. "Threats aren't going to cut it with me, Dakota."

"No?" He shifted gears smoothly. His hand came

back to her face, but lightly now, a skim of knuckles along a cheekbone that had her blinking in shock before her eyes narrowed. "You want a different approach?"

His fingers trailed down her throat, down the center of her body and back, before sliding around to cup her neck. His mouth hovered, one hot breath away from hers.

"Don't even think about it," she warned.

"Too late." His lips curved, and his eyes stared straight into hers. "I've been thinking about it ever since you swaggered up the apartment steps in front of me."

No, he'd been thinking about it, he realized, since Ralph shoved her photo at him. But he'd consider that later.

He skimmed his mouth over hers, drew back fractionally. He'd expected her to cringe away or fight. God knew he was ruthlessly pushing all those female fear buttons. It was deplorable, but he'd consider that later, as well. He just wanted the pressure to work, to get her to spill before they both got killed. And if he got a little twisted pleasure out of the whole thing, well, hell, he had his flaws.

But she didn't fight and she didn't cringe. She didn't move a muscle, just kept those goddess-green eyes lasered on his. A dark, primitive thrill rippled down to his loins.

What was one more sin on his back, he thought, and, clamping his hand on her free one, he took a long, deep gulp of her.

It was all heat, primitive as tribal drums. No thought, no reason, all instinct. That surprisingly lush mouth gave under his, so he dived deeper. A rumble of pure male triumph sounded in his throat as he moved into her, plunging his tongue between those full, inviting lips, sinking into that long, tough body, fisting his hand in that cap of flame-colored hair.

His mind shut off like a shattered lamp. He forgot it was a con, a ploy to intimidate, forgot he was a civilized man. Forgot she was a job, a puzzle, a stranger. And knew only that she was his for the taking.

His hand closed greedily over her breast, his thumb and forefinger tugging at the nipple that pressed hard against the thin cotton of her shirt. She moved under him, arched to him. And the blood pounded like thunder in his brain.

She moved fast, all but twisting his ear from his head while her teeth clamped down like a bear trap on his bottom lip.

He yelped, jerked back, and, certain she would saw off a chunk of him, pinched her chin hard until she let him loose. He pressed the back of his hand to his throbbing lip, scowled at the blood he saw on it when he took it away.

"Damn it."

"Pig." She was vibrating now, scrambling to her knees on the bed to take another swipe at him, swearing when her reach fell short. "Pervert."

He spared her one murderous look, then turned on his heel. The bathroom door slammed shut behind him. She heard water running. And, closing her eyes, she sank back and let the shudders come.

My God, dear God, she thought, pressing a hand to her face. She'd lost her mind.

Had she fought him? No. Had she been filled with outrage, with disgust? No.

She'd enjoyed it.

She rocked herself, berated herself, and damned Jack Dakota to hell.

She'd let him kiss her. There was no pretending otherwise. She'd stared into those dangerous gray eyes, felt the zip of an electric current when that cocky mouth brushed over hers.

And she'd wanted him.

Her muscles had gone lax, her breasts had tingled, and her blood had begun to swim. She'd let him kiss her without a murmur of protest. She'd kissed him back, without a thought for the consequences.

M. J. O'Leary, she thought, wincing, tough gal, who prided herself on always being in control, who could flip a two-hundred-pound man onto his back and have her foot on his throat in a heartbeat—confident, kick-butt M.J.—had melted into a puddle of mindless lust.

And he'd tied her up, he'd gagged her, he had her handcuffed to a bed in some cheap motel. Wanting him even for an instant made her as much of a pervert as he was.

Thank God she'd snapped out of it. It didn't matter that bone-deep fear of her feelings had been the motivation for stopping him. The fact was, she had stopped him—and she knew she'd been an instant away from letting him do whatever he wanted to do.

She was very much afraid that if she'd had both hands free, she would have flipped him onto his back. Then ripped off his clothes.

It was the shock, she told herself. Even a woman who prided herself on being able to handle anything that came her way was entitled to go a little loopy with shock under certain circumstances.

Now she had to put this aberration behind her and figure out what to do.

The facts were few, but they were clear. She had to contact Bailey. Whatever her friend's purpose in sending the stone, Bailey couldn't have had any idea just how dangerous the act would be. She'd had her reasons, M.J. was sure, and she thought it was likely to have been one of Bailey's rare acts of impulse and defiance.

She didn't intend for Bailey to pay the price for it.

What had Bailey done with the other two stones? Did she have them, or... Oh God.

She dropped back weakly on the bricklike pillow. She would have sent one to Grace. It had to be. It was logical, and Bailey was nothing if not logical. There'd been three stones, and she'd sent one to M.J. So it followed that she'd kept one, and sent the other to the only other person in the world she'd trust with such a responsibility.

Grace Fontaine. The three of them had been close as sisters since college. Bailey, quiet, studious and serious. Grace, rich, stunning and wild. They'd roomed together for four years at Radcliffe and stayed close since. Bailey moving into the family business, M.J. following tradition and opening her own bar, and Grace doing whatever she could to shock her wealthy, conservative and disapproving relatives.

If one of them was in trouble, they were all in trouble. She had to warn them.

She would have to escape from Jack Dakota. Or she'd have to use him.

But how much, she asked herself, did she dare trust him?

In the bathroom, Jack studied his mutilated lip in the mirror. He'd probably have a scar. Well, he admitted, he deserved it. He *had* been a pig and a pervert.

Not that she was entirely innocent, either, lying there on the bed with that just-try-it-buster look in her eyes.

And hadn't she pressed that long, tight body to his, opened that soft, sexy mouth, arched those neat, narrow hips?

Pig. He scrubbed his hands over his face. What choice had he given her?

Dropping his hands, he looked at himself in the mirror, looked dead-on, and admitted he hadn't wanted to give her a choice.

He'd just wanted her.

Well, he wasn't an animal. He could control himself, he could think, he could reason. And that was just what he was going to do.

He'd probably have a scar, he thought again, grimly, as he touched a fingertip gingerly to his swollen lip. Just let that be a lesson to you, Dakota. He jerked his head in a nod at the reflection in the spotty mirror. If you can't trust yourself, you sure as hell can't trust her.

When he came out, she was frowning at the hideous drapes on the window. He glared at her. She glared back. Saying nothing, he sat in the single ratty chair, crossed his feet at the ankles and tuned into the movie.

Hercules was over. He'd probably triumphed. In his place was a Japanese science-fiction flick with an incredibly poorly produced monster lizard who was currently smashing a high-speed train. Hordes of extras were screaming in terror.

They watched awhile, as the military came rushing in with large guns that had virtually no effect on the giant mutant lizard. A small man in a combat helmet was devoured. His chickenhearted comrades ran for their lives.

M.J. found the candy bar from her purse that Jack had tossed her earlier, broke off a chunk and ate it contemplatively as the lizard king from outer space lumbered toward Tokyo to wreak reptilian havoc.

"Can I have my water?" she asked in scrupulously polite tones.

He got up, fetched it out of her bag, handed it over.

"Thanks." She took one long sip, waited until

he'd settled again. "What's your fee?" she demanded.

He took another soda out of his cooler. Wished it was a beer. "For?"

"What you do." She shrugged. "Say I had skipped out on bail. What do you get for bringing me back?"

"Depends. Why?"

She rolled her eyes. "Depends on what?"

"On how much bail you'd skipped out on."

She was silent for a moment as she considered. The lizard demolished a tall building with many innocent occupants. "What was it I was supposed to have done?"

"Shot your lover—the accountant. I believe his name was Hank."

"Very funny." She broke off another hunk of chocolate and, when Jack held out a hand, reluctantly shared. "How much were you going to get for me?"

"More than you're worth."

Now she sighed. "I'm going to make you a deal, Jack, but I'm a businesswoman, and I don't make them blind. What's your fee?"

Interesting, he thought, and drummed his fingers on the arm of the chair. "For you, sugar, considering what you're carrying in that suitcase you call a purse, adding in what Ralph offered me to turn you over to the goons?" He thought it over. "A hundred large."

She didn't bat an eye. "I appreciate you trying to lighten the situation with an attempt at wry humor.

A hundred K for a man who can't even take out a single hired thug by himself is laughable—''

"Who said I couldn't take him out?" His pride leaped up and bit him. "I *did* take him out, sugar. Him and his cannon, and you haven't bothered to thank me for it."

"Oh, excuse me. It must have slipped my mind while I was being dragged around and handcuffed. How rude. And you didn't take him out, I did. But regardless," she continued, holding up her free hand like a traffic cop, "now that we've had our little joke, let's try to be serious. I'll give you a thousand to work with me on this."

"A thousand?" He flashed that quick, dangerous grin. "Sister, there isn't enough money in the world to tempt me to work with you. But for a hundred K, I'll get you out of the jam you're in."

"In the first place—" she drew up her legs, sat lotus-style "—I'm not your sister, and I'm not your sugar. If you have to refer to me, use my name."

"You don't have a name, you have initials."

"In the second place," she said, ignoring him, "if a man like you got his hands on a hundred thousand, he'd just lose it in Vegas or pour it down some stripper's cleavage. Since I don't intend for that to happen to my money, I'm offering you a thousand." She smiled at him. "With that, you can have yourself a nice weekend at the beach with a keg of imported beer."

"It's considerate of you to look out for my welfare, but you're not really in the position to negotiate terms here. You want help, it'll cost you.''

She didn't know if she wanted his help. The fact was, she wasn't at all sure why she was wrangling with him over a fee. Under the circumstances, she felt she could promise him any amount without any obligation to pay up if and when the time came.

But it was the principle of the thing.

"Five thousand—and you follow orders."

"Seventy-five, and I don't ever follow orders."

"Five." She set her teeth. "Take it or leave it."

"I'll leave it." Casually he picked up the stone again, held it up, studied it. "And take this with me." He rose, patted his back pocket. "And maybe I'll call the cops on your fancy little phone after I'm clear."

She fisted her fingers, flexed them. She didn't want to involve the police, not until she'd contacted Bailey. Nor could she risk him following through on his threat to simply take the stone.

"Fifty thousand." She bit the words off like raw meat. "That's all I'll be able to come up with. Most everything I've got's tied up in my business."

He cocked a brow. "The finder's fee on this little bauble's got to be worth more than fifty."

"I didn't steal the damn thing. It doesn't belong to me. It's—" She broke off, clamped her mouth shut.

He started to sit on the edge of the bed again, remembered what had happened before, and chose the arm of the chair. "Who does it belong to, M.J.?"

"I'm not spilling my guts to you. For all I know you're as big a creep as the one who broke down my door. You could be a thief, a murderer."

He cocked that scarred eyebrow. "Which is why I've robbed and murdered you."

"The day's young."

"Let me point out the obvious. I'm the only one around."

"That doesn't inspire confidence." She brooded a moment. How far did she dare use him? she wondered. And how much did she dare tell him?

"If you want my help," he said, as if reading her mind, "then I need facts, details and names."

"I'm not giving you names." She shook her head slowly. "That's out until I talk to the other people involved. And as for facts and details, I don't have many."

"Give me what you do have."

She studied him again. No, she didn't trust him, not nearly as far as she could throw him. If she ever got the opportunity. But she had to start somewhere. "Unlock me."

He shook his head. "Let's just leave things as they are for the moment." But he rose, walked over and shut off the television. "Where'd you get the stone, M.J.?"

She hesitated another instant. Trust wasn't the issue, she decided. He might help, if in no other way than just by providing her with a sounding board. "A friend sent it to me. Overnight courier. I just got it yesterday."

"Where did it come from?"

"Originally from Asia Minor, I believe." She shrugged off his hiss of annoyance. "I'm not telling you where it was sent from, but I will tell you there had to be a good reason. My friend's too honest to steal a handshake. All I know is it was sent, with a note that said for me to keep it with me at all times, and not to tell anyone until my friend had a chance to explain."

Abruptly she pressed a hand to her stomach and the arrogance died out of her voice. "My friend's in trouble. It's got to be terrible trouble. I have to call."

"No calls."

"Look, Jack—"

"No calls," he repeated. "Whoever's after you might be after your pal. His phone could be tapped, which would lead them back to you. Which leads them to me, so no calls. Now how did your honest friend happen to get his hands on a blue diamond that makes the Hope look like a prize in a box of Cracker Jack?"

"In a perfectly legitimate manner." Stalling, she combed her fingers through her hair. He thought her friend was male—why not leave it that way?

"Look, I'm not getting into all of that. All I'm going to tell you is he was supposed to have his hands on it. Look, let me tell you about the stone. It's one of three. At one time they were part of an altar set up to an ancient Roman god. Mithraism was one of the major religions of the Roman Empire—"

"The Three Stars of Mithra," he murmured, and

had her eyeing him first in shock, then with suspicion.

"How do you know about the Three Stars?"

"I read about them in the dentist's office," he murmured. Now, when he picked up the stone, it wasn't simply with admiration, it was with awe. "It was supposed to be a myth. The Three Stars, set in the golden triangle and held in the hands of the god of light."

"It's not a myth," M.J. told him. "The Smithsonian acquired the Stars through a contact in Europe just a couple months ago. My friend said the museum wanted to keep the acquisition quiet until the diamonds were verified."

"And assessed," he thought aloud. "Insured and under tight security."

"They were supposed to be under security," M.J. told him, and he answered with a soft laugh.

"Doesn't look like it worked, does it? The diamonds represent love, knowledge and generosity." His eyes narrowed as he contemplated the ancient stone. "I wonder which this one is?"

"I couldn't say." She continued to stare at him, fascinated. He'd gone from tough guy to scholar in the blink of an eye. "But apparently you know as much about it as I do."

"I know about Mithraism," he said easily. "It predates and parallels Christianity. Mankind's always looked for a kind and just god." His shoulders moved as he turned the stone in his hand. "Mankind doesn't always get what it wants. And I know the

legend of the Three Stars. It was said the god held
the triangle for centuries, and holding it tended the
world. Then it was lost, or looted, or sank with At-
lantis."

For his own pleasure, he switched on the lamp,
watched the stone explode with power in the dingy
light. "More likely it just ended up in the treasure
room of some corrupt Roman procurer." He traced
the facets with his thumbs. "It's something people
would kill for. Or die for," he murmured. "Some
legends have it in Cleopatra's tomb, others have
Merlin casing it in crystal and holding it in trust until
Arthur's return. Others say the god himself hurled
them into the sky and wept at man's ignorance. But
the smart money was that they'd simply been stolen
and separated."

He looked up, over the stone and into her eyes.
"Worth a fortune singly, and within the triangle,
worth immortality."

Yes, she could admit he fascinated her, the way
that deep, all-man voice had cooled into professorial
tones. And the way he stroked the gleaming diamond
as a man might stroke a woman's gleaming flesh.

But she shook her head over the last statement.
"You don't believe that."

"No, but that's the legend, isn't it? Whoever holds
the triangle, with the Stars in place, gains the power
of the god, and his immortality. But not necessarily
his compassion. People have killed for less. A hell
of a lot less."

He set the stone on the table between them, where

it glowed with quiet fire. It had all changed now, he realized. The stakes had just flown sky-high, and the odds mirrored them.

"You're in a hell of a spot, M.J. Whoever's after this won't think twice about taking your head with it." He rubbed his chin, his fingers dancing over the shallow dimple. "And my head's awfully damn close to yours just now."

He couldn't believe how poor his luck was. His own mistake, he told himself as he calmed himself with Mozart and Moët. Because he tried to keep his distance from events, he'd had to count on others to handle his business.

Incompetents, one and all, he thought, and soothed himself by stroking the pelt of a sable coat that had once graced the shoulder of Czarina Alexandra.

To think he'd enjoyed the irony of having a bounty hunter track down the annoying Ms. O'Leary. It would have been simpler to have her snatched from her apartment or place of business. But he'd preferred finesse and, again, the distance.

The bounty hunter would have been blamed for her abduction, and her death. Such men were violent by nature, unpredictable. The police would have closed the case with little thought or effort.

Now she was on the run, and most certainly had the stone in her possession.

She would turn up, he thought, taking slow, even breaths. She would certainly contact her friends before too much longer. He'd been assured they were admirably loyal to each other.

He was a man who appreciated loyalty.

And when Ms. O'Leary attempted to contact her friends—one who had vanished, the other out of reach—he would have her.

And the stone.

With her, he had no doubt he would acquire the other two stars.

After all, he thought with a pleasant smile. Bailey James was reputed to be a good friend, a compassionate and intelligent woman. Intelligent enough, he mused, to have uncovered her stepbrothers' attempt to copy the Stars, smart enough to thwart them before they had made good on delivery.

Well, that, too, would be dealt with.

He was sure Bailey would be loyal to her friend, compassionate enough to put her friend first. And her loyalty and compassion would deliver the stones to him without much more delay.

In exchange for the life of M. J. O'Leary.

He had spent many years of his life in search of the Three Stars. He had invested much of his great wealth. And had taken many lives. Now they were almost in his hands. So close, he thought, so very close, his fingers tingled with anticipation.

And when he held them, fit them into the triangle, set them on the altar he'd had built for them, he would have the ultimate power. Immortality.

Then, of course, he would kill the women.

A fitting sacrifice, he reflected, to a god.

Chapter 4

He'd left her alone. Now she had to consider the matter of trust. Should she believe he'd just go out, pick up food and come back? He hadn't trusted her to stay, M.J. mused, rattling the handcuffs.

And she had to admit he'd gauged her well. She'd have been out the door like a shot. Not because she was afraid of him. She'd considered all the facts, all her instincts, and she no longer believed he'd hurt her. He would have done so already.

She'd seen the way he dealt with the gorilla who broke in her door. True, he'd had his hands full, but he'd handled himself with speed, strength, and an admirable streak of mean.

It galled to admit it, but she knew he'd held back when he tangled with her. Not that it excused him trussing her up and tossing her in some cheap motel room, but if she was going to be fair-minded, she had to say he could have done considerable damage to her during their quick, sweaty bout if he'd wanted to.

And all he'd really bruised was her pride.

He had a brain—which had surprised her. That was, she supposed, a generalizing-from-a-first-impression mistake she'd fallen into because of his looks, and that sheer in-your-face physicality. But in addition to the street smarts she would have expected from his type, it appeared Jack Dakota had an intellect. A good one.

And she didn't believe he did his reading in the dentist's office. A guy didn't read about ancient religions while he was waiting to have his teeth cleaned. So, she had to conclude there was more to him than she'd originally assumed. All she had to do was decide whether that was an advantage, or a disadvantage.

Now that she'd calmed down a little, she was certain that he wasn't going to push himself on her sexually, either. She'd have given odds that little interlude had shaken him as much as it had shaken her. It had been, she was sure, a misstep on his part. Intimidate the woman, flex the testosterone, and she'll tell you whatever you want to know.

It hadn't worked. All it had done was make them both itchy.

Damn, the man could kiss.

But she was getting off track, she reminded herself, and scowled at the ridiculous movie he'd left blaring on the television.

No, she wasn't afraid of him, but she was afraid of the situation. Which meant she didn't want to sit here on her butt and do nothing. Action was her style. Whether the action was wise or not wasn't the point. The doing was.

Shifting to her knees, she peered at the handcuffs, turning her wrist this way and that, flexing her hand as if she were an escape artist preparing to launch into her latest trick.

She tested the rungs on the headboard and found them distressingly firm.

They didn't make cheap hotels like they used to, she thought with a sigh. And wished for a hairpin, a nail file, a hammer.

All she found in the sticky drawer of the night-stand was a torn phone book and a linty wedge of hard candy.

He'd taken her purse with him, and though she knew she wouldn't find that hairpin, nail file or hammer inside, she still resented the lack of it.

She could scream, of course. She could shout down the roof, and endure the humiliation if some-one actually paid any attention to the sounds of distress.

And that wouldn't get her out of the cuffs, unless someone called a locksmith. Or the cops.

She took a deep breath, struggled for the right avenue of escape. She was sick with worry for Bailey and Grace, desperate to reassure herself that they were both well.

If she did go to the police, what kind of trouble would Bailey be in? She had, technically, taken possession of a fortune. Would the authorities be understanding, or would they slap Bailey in a cell?

That, M.J. wouldn't risk. Not yet. Not as long as she felt it was remotely possible to even the odds. And to do that, she had to know what the hell she was up against.

Which again meant getting out of the room.

She was considering gnawing at the headboard with her teeth when Jack unlocked the door. He flashed a quick smile at her, one that told her he had her thoughts pegged.

"Honey, I'm home."

"You're a laugh riot, Dakota. My sides are aching."

"You make quite a picture cuffed to that bed, M.J." He set down two white take-out bags. "A lesser man would be toying with impure notions right about now."

It was her turn to smile, wickedly. "You already did. And you'll probably have a scar on your bottom lip."

"Yeah." He rubbed his thumb gingerly over the wound. It still stung. "I'd say I deserved it, but you were cooperating initially."

That stung, too. The truth often did. "You go right on thinking that, Jack." She all but purred it. "I'm sure an ego like yours requires regular delusions."

"Sugar, I know a delusion from a lip lock. But we've got more important things to do than discuss your attraction for me." Pleased with that last sally, he reached into one of the bags. "Burgers."

The smell hit her like a fist, right in the empty stomach. Her mouth watered. "So are we going to hole up here like a couple of escaped convicts—" she rattled her chain for emphasis "—and eat greasy food?"

"You bet." He handed her a burger and took out an order of fries designed to clog the arteries and improve the mood. "I think better when I'm eating."

Companionably, he stretched out beside her, back against the headboard, legs extended, food on his lap. "We've got us a serious problem here."

"If *we've* got us a serious problem here, why am I the only one with handcuffs?"

He loved the sarcastic edge in her voice, and he wondered what was wrong with him. "Because you'd have done something stupid if I hadn't left you secured. I'm looking out for my investment." He gestured with the rest of his burger. "And that's you, sugar."

"I can look out for myself. And if I'm hiring you, then you should be taking orders. The first order is unlock these damn things."

"I'll get to it, once we set up the ground rules." He popped open a paper package of salt, dribbled it on the fries. "I've been thinking."

"Well then." She munched bitterly on an overcooked burger between two slices of slightly stale bun. "Why am I worried? You've been thinking."

"You've got a sarcastic mouth. But I like that about you." He handed her a tiny paper napkin. "You got ketchup on your chin. Now, somebody put the pressure on Ralph—enough that Ralph falsified official paperwork and put my butt in a sling. He wouldn't have done it for money—not that Ralph doesn't like money," Jack continued. "But he wouldn't risk his license, or risk me coming after him, for a few bucks. So he was saving his skin."

"And since Ralph is a pillar of the community, no doubt, this narrows down the list?"

"It means it was somebody with punch, somebody who wasn't afraid old Ralph would tip me off or go to the cops. Somebody who wanted you taken out. Who knows you've got the rock?"

"Nobody, except the person who sent it to me." She frowned at her burger. "And possibly one other."

"If more than one person knows a secret, it isn't a secret. How did your friend get the diamond, M.J.? You can't keep dancing around the data here."

"I'll tell you after I clear it with my friend. I have to make a phone call."

"No calls."

"You called Ralph," she pointed out.

"I took a chance, and we were mobile. You're not making any calls until I know the score. The diamond was shipped just yesterday," he mused. "They tagged you fast."

"Which means they tagged my friend." Her stomach turned over. "Jack, please. I have to call. I have to know."

The emotion choking her voice both weakened and annoyed him. He stared into her eyes. "How much does he mean to you?"

She started to correct him, then just shook her head. "Everything. No one in the world means more to me."

"Lucky guy."

It wasn't the response she'd wanted or expected. Fueled by frustration and fears, she grabbed his shirt. "What the hell's wrong with you? Someone tried to kill us. How can we just sit here?"

"That's just why we're sitting here. We let them chase their tails awhile. Your friend's on his own for now. And since I can't picture you falling for some jerk who can't handle himself, he should be fine."

"You don't understand anything." She sat back, dragged her fingers through her hair. "God, this is a mess. I should be getting ready to go in to work now, and instead I'm stuck here with you. I'm supposed to be behind the stick tonight."

"You tend bar?" He lifted a brow. "I thought you owned the place."

"That's right, I own the place." It was a source of pride. "I like tending bar. You have a problem with that?"

"Nope." Since the topic had distracted her, he followed it. "Are you any good?"

"Nobody complains."

"How'd you get into the business?" When she eyed him owlishly, he shrugged. "Come on, a little conversation over a meal can't hurt. We got time to kill."

That wasn't all she wanted to kill, but the rest would have to wait. "I'm a fourth-generation pub owner. My great-grandfather ran his own public house in Dublin. My grandfather immigrated to New York and worked behind the stick in his own pub. He passed it to my father when he moved to Florida. I practically grew up behind the bar."

"What part of New York?"

"West Side, Seventy-ninth and Columbus."

"O'Leary's." The grin came quick and close to dreamy. "Lots of dark wood and lots of brass. Live Irish music on Saturday nights. And they build the finest Guinness this side of the Atlantic."

She eyed him again, intrigued despite herself. "You've been there?"

"I downed many a pint in O'Leary's. That would have been ten years ago, more or less." He'd been in college then, he remembered. Working his way through courses in law and literature and trying to make up his mind who the devil he was. "I was up there tracing a skip about three years ago. Stopped in. Nothing had changed, not even the scars on that old pine bar."

It made her sentimental—couldn't be helped. "Nothing changes at O'Leary's."

"I swear the same two guys were sitting on the

same stools at the end of the bar—smoking cigars, reading the *Racing Form* and drinking Irish.''

"Callahan and O'Neal." It made her smile. "They'll die on those stools."

"And your father. Pat O'Leary. Son of a bitch." Steeped in the haze of memory, he shut his eyes. "That big, wide Irish face and wiry shock of red hair, with a voice straight out of a Cagney movie."

"Yeah, that's Pop," she murmured, only more sentimental.

"You know, when I walked in—it had been at least six years since I'd walked out—your father grinned at me. 'How are you this evening, college boy?' he said to me, and took a pint glass and starting building my beer."

"You went to college?"

His hazy pleasure dimmed considerably at the shock in her voice. He opened one eye. "So?"

"So, you don't look like the college type." She shrugged and went back to her burger. "I build a damn good Guinness myself. Could use one now."

"Me too. Maybe later. So this friend of yours, how long have you known him?"

"My friend and I go back to our own college days. There's no one I trust more, if that's what you're getting at."

"Maybe you ought to rethink it. Just consider," he said when her eyes fired. "The Three Stars are a big temptation, for anyone. So maybe he was tempted, maybe he got in over his head."

"No, it doesn't play like that. but I think someone

else might have, and if my friend found out about
it…" She pressed her lips together. "If you wanted
to protect those stones, to make certain they weren't
stolen, didn't fall as a group into the wrong hands,
what would you do?"

"It isn't a matter of what I'd do," he pointed out,
"but what he'd do."

"Separate them," M.J. said. "Pass them on to
people you could trust without question. People who
would go to the wall for you, because you'd do the
same for them. Without question."

"Absolute trust, absolute loyalty?" He balled his
napkin, two-pointed it into the waste can. "I can't
buy it."

"Then I'm sorry for you," she murmured. "Because you can't buy it. It just is. Don't you have
anyone who'd go to the wall for you, Jack?"

"No. And there's no one I'd go to the wall for."
For the first time in his life, it bothered him to realize
it. He scooted down, closed his eyes. "I'm taking a
nap."

"You're taking a what?"

"A nap. You'd be smart to do the same."

"How can you possibly sleep at a time like this?"

"Because I'm tired." His voice was edgy. "And
because I don't think I'm going to get much sleep
once we get started. We've got a couple hours before
sundown."

"And what happens at sundown?"

"It gets dark," he said, and tuned her out.

She couldn't believe it. The man had shut down

like a machine switched off—like a hypnotist's subject at the snap of a finger. Like a... She scowled when she ran out of analogies.

At least he didn't snore.

Well, this was just fine, she fumed. This was just dandy. What was she supposed to do while he had his little lie-me-down?

M.J. nibbled on the last of her fries, frowned at the TV screen, where the giant lizard was just meeting his violent end. The cable channel had promised more where that came from on its Marathon Monsters and Heroes Holiday Weekend Festival.

Oh, goody.

She lay in the darkened room, considering her options. And, considering, fell asleep.

And, sleeping, dreamed of monsters and heroes and a blue diamond that pulsed like a living heart.

Jack woke wrapped in female. He smelled her first, a tang, just a little sharp, of lemony soap. Clean, fresh, and simple.

He heard her—the slow, even, relaxed breathing. Felt the quiet intimacy of shared sleep. His blood began to stir even before he felt her.

Long, limber limbs. A shapely yard of leg was tossed over his own. One well-toned arm, with skin as smooth as new cream, was flung over his chest. Her head was settled companionably on his shoulder.

M.J. was a cuddler, he realized, and smiled to himself. Who'd have thought it? Before he could talk himself out of it, he lifted a hand, brushed it lightly over her tousled cap of hair. Bright silk, he mused. It was quite a contrast to all that angled toughness.

She sure had style. His kind of style, he decided, and wondered what direction they might have taken if he just walked into her pub one night and put some moves on her.

She'd have kicked him out on his butt, he thought, and grinned. What a woman.

It was too bad, too damn bad, that he didn't have time to try out those moves. Because he really wanted another taste of her.

And because he did, he slid out from under her, stood and stretched out the kinks while she shifted and tried to find comfort. She rolled onto her back and flung her free hand over her head.

The restless animal inside him stirred.

He grabbed it in a choke hold and reminded himself that he was, occasionally, a civilized man. Civilized men didn't climb onto a sleeping woman and dive in.

But they could think about it.

Since it would be safer all around to think about it at a distance, he went into the bathroom, splashed cold water on his face and considered his next move.

In dreams, she was holding the stone in her hand, wondering at it, as streams of sunlight danced through the canopy of trees. Instead of penetrating the stone, the rays bounced off, creating a flashing whirl of beauty that stung the eyes and burned the soul.

It was hers to hold, if not to keep. The answers were there, secreted inside, if only she knew where to look.

From somewhere came the growl of a beast, low and feral. She turned toward it, rather than away, the stone protected in the fist of her hand, her other raised to defend.

Something moved slyly in the brush, hidden, waiting, searching. Hunting.

Then he was there, astride a massive black horse. At his side was a sword of dull silver, its width a thick slab of violence. His gray eyes were granite-hard, and as dangerous as any beast that slunk over the ground. He held a hand down to her, and there was challenge in that slow smile.

Danger ahead. Danger behind.

She stepped forward, clasped hands with him and let him pull her up on the gleaming black horse. The horse reared high, trumpeted. When they rode, they rode fast. The blood beating in her head had nothing to do with fear, and everything to do with triumph.

She came awake with her heart pounding and her blood high. She was in the dim, cramped motel room, with Jack shaking her shoulder roughly.

"What? What?"

"Nap's over." He considered kissing her awake, risking her fist in his face. But it would be too distracting. "We've got places to go."

"Where?" She struggled to shake off sleep, and the silky remnants of the dream.

"To visit a friend." He unlocked the cuffs from

the headboard, snapped them on his own wrist, linking M.J. to him.

"You have a friend?"

"Ah, she's awake now." He pulled her outside, into a misty dusk that still pulsed with heat. "Get in and slide over," he instructed when he opened the driver's side door.

She was still groggy enough that she obeyed without question. But by the time he'd started the engine, her wits were back. "Look, Jack, these handcuffs have got to go."

"I don't know, I kind of like them this way. Did you ever see that movie with Tony Curtis and Sidney Poitier? Great flick."

"We're not escaped cons running for a train here, Dakota. If we're going to have a business relationship, there has to be an element of trust."

"Sugar, you don't trust me any more than I trust you." He steered out of the pitted lot, kept to the speed limit. "Look at it this way." He lifted his hand, causing hers to jerk. "We're both in the same boat. And I could have just left you back there."

She drummed her fingers on her knee. "Why didn't you?"

"I thought about it," he admitted. "I could move faster without you along. But I'd rather keep my eye on you. And if things go wrong and I can't get back, I'd hate for you to have to explain why you're cuffed to the bed of a cheap motel."

"Damn considerate of you."

"I thought so. Though it's your fault I'm flying blind. It'd be easier if you'd fill in the blanks."

"Think of it as a challenge."

"Oh, I do. It, and you." He slanted her a look. "What's this guy got, M.J.? This *friend* of yours you'd risk so much for?"

She looked out her window, thought of Bailey. Then pushed the thought aside. Worry for Bailey only brought the fear back, and fear clouded the mind and made it sluggish.

"You wouldn't understand love, would you, Jack?" Her voice was quiet, without its usual edge, and her gaze passed over his face in a slow search. "The kind that doesn't ask questions, doesn't require favors or have limits."

"No." Inside the emptiness her words brought him curled an edgy fist of envy. "I'd say if you don't ask questions or have limits, you're a fool."

"And you're no fool."

"Under the circumstances, you should be grateful I'm not. I'll get you out of this, M.J. Then you'll owe me fifty thousand."

"You know your priorities," she said with a sneer.

"Yeah, money smooths out a lot of bumps on the road. And I say before you pay me off we end up in bed again. Only this time it won't be to take a nap."

She turned toward him fully, and ignored the quick pulse of excitement in her gut. "Dakota, the only way I'll end up in the sack with you is if you hand-cuff me again."

There was that smile, slow, insolent, damnably attractive. "Well, that would be interesting, wouldn't it?"

Wanting to make time, he swung onto the interstate, headed north. And he promised himself that not only would he get her into bed, but she wouldn't think of another man when he did.

"You're heading back to D.C."

"That's right. We've got some business there." In the glare of oncoming headlights, his face was grim.

He took a roundabout route, circling, cruising past his objective, winding his way back, until he was satisfied none of the cars parked on the block were occupied.

There was pedestrian traffic, as well. He'd sized it up by his second pass. Deals were being made, he mused. And that kind of business kept people moving.

"Nice neighborhood," she commented, watching a drunk stumble out of a liquor store with a brown paper sack. "Just charming. Yours?"

"Ralph's. We're only a couple blocks from the courthouse." He cruised past a prostitute who was well off the usual stroll and pulled around the corner. "He likes the location."

It was an area, she knew, that even the most fearless cabbies preferred to avoid. An area where life was often worth less than the spit on the sidewalk, and those who valued theirs locked their doors tight before sundown and waited for morning.

Here, the graffiti smeared on the crumbling buildings wasn't an art form. It was a threat.

She heard someone swearing viciously, then the sound of breaking glass. "A man of taste and refinement, your friend Ralph."

"Former friend." He took her hand, obliging her to slide across the seat when he climbed out.

"That you, Dakota? That you?" A man slipped out of the shadows of a doorway. His eyes were fire red and skittish as a whipped dog's. He ran the back of his hand over his mouth as he shambled forward in battered high-tops and an overcoat that had to be stifling in the midsummer heat.

"Yeah, Freddie. How's it going?"

"Been better. Been better, Jack, you know?" His eyes passed over M.J., then moved on. "Been better," he said again.

"Yeah, I know." Jack reached in his front pocket for the bills he'd already placed there. "You could use a hot meal."

"A hot meal." Freddie stared at the bills, moistened his lips. "Sure could do with a hot meal, all right."

"You seen Ralph?"

"Ain't." Freddie's shaky fingers reached for the money, clamped on. He blinked up when Jack continued to hold the bills. "Ain't," he repeated. "Musta closed up early. It's a holiday, the Fourth of Ju-ly. Damn kids been setting off firecrackers already. Can't tell them from gunshots. Damn kids."

"When's the last time you saw Ralph?"

"I dunno. Yesterday?" He looked at Jack for approval. "Yesterday, probably. I've been here awhile, but I ain't seen him. And his place is locked up."

"Have you seen anybody else who doesn't belong here?"

"Her." Freddie pointed at M.J. and smiled. "She don't."

"Besides her."

"Nope. Nobody." The voice went whiny. "I sure been better, Jack, you know."

"Yeah." Without bothering to sigh, Jack turned the money loose. "Get lost, Freddie."

"Yeah, okay." And he hurried down the street, around the corner.

"He's not going to buy food," M.J. murmured. "You know what he's going to buy with that."

"You can't save the world. Sometimes you can't even save a little piece of it. But maybe he won't mug anybody tonight, or get himself shot trying to." Jack shrugged. "He's been dead since the first time he picked up a needle. Nothing I can do about it."

"Then why do you feel so lousy about it?" She lifted a brow when he looked down at her. "It's all over your face, Dakota."

"He used to have a family" was all he said by way of an answer. "Let's go." He led her up the street, then ducked down the side of a building. To her surprise, he unlocked the cuffs. "You've got more sense than to take off in this neighborhood." He smiled. "And I've got your rock locked in the trunk of my car."

"On a street like this, you'll be lucky if your car's still there when you get back around."

"They know my car. Nobody'll mess with it." Then he turned—whirled, really—and made her jolt as he slammed two vicious kicks into a dull gray door.

She heard wood splinter, and pursed her lips in appreciation as the door gave way on the third try. "Nice job."

"Thanks. And if Ralph didn't get cute and change the code, we're in business." He stepped inside, scanned an alarm box beside the broken door. With quick fingers he stabbed numbers.

"How do you know his code?"

"I make it my business to know things. Move aside." With a strength she had to admire, he hauled the broken door up, muscled it back into place. "Ralph should have gone for steel. Too cheap."

He flicked on the lights, scanned the tiny space that was crammed with file boxes and smelled of must. M.J. watched a mouse scamper out of sight.

"Charming. I'm very impressed with your associates so far, Dakota. Would this be his secretary's year off?"

"Ralph doesn't have a secretary, either. He's a big believer in low overhead. Office is through here."

"I can't wait." Wary of rodents and anything else with more than two legs, she watched her step as she followed him. "This is what they call nighttime breaking and entering, isn't it?"

"Cops have a name for everything." He paused

with his hand on a doorknob, glanced over his shoulder. "If you wanted someone who'd knock politely on the front door, you wouldn't be with me."

She lifted her arm, rattled the dangling handcuffs. "Remember these?"

He only shook his head. "You wouldn't be with me," he repeated, and opened the door.

She sucked in her breath, but it was the only sound she made. Later, he would remember that and appreciate her grit and her control. The backwash of light from the anteroom spilled into the closet-size office.

Gunmetal-gray file cabinets, scarred and dented, lined two walls. Papers spilled out of the open drawers, littered the floor, fluttered on the desk under the breeze of a whining electric fan.

Blood was everywhere.

The smell of it roiled in her stomach, had her clamping her teeth and swallowing hard. But her voice was steady enough when she spoke.

"That would be Ralph?"

Chapter 5

It had been a messy job, Jack thought. If it had been pros, they hadn't bothered to be quick or neat. But then, there'd been no reason for either. Ralph was still tied to the chair.

Or what was left of him was.

"You can wait in the back," Jack told her.

"I don't think so." She wasn't a stranger to violence. A girl didn't grow up in a bar and not see blood spilled from time to time.

But she'd never seen anything like this. As realistic as she considered herself, she hadn't really believed it was possible for one human being to inflict this kind of horror on another.

She kept her eyes on the wall, but stepped in beside him. "What do you think they were after?"

"The same thing I am. Anything that leads back

to whoever used Ralph to set us up. Stupid son of a bitch.'' His voice softened all at once, with what could only have been termed regret. ''Why didn't he run?''

''Maybe he didn't have the chance.'' Her stomach was settling, but she continued to take small, shallow breaths. ''We have to call the police.''

''Sure, we'll call 911, then we'll wait and explain ourselves. From the inside of a cell.'' Crouching down, he began shuffling through papers.

''Jack, for God's sake, the man's been murdered.''

''He won't be any less dead if we call the cops, will he? Never could figure out Ralph's filing system.''

''Haven't you got any feelings at all? You knew him.''

''I haven't got time for feelings.'' And since they were trying to surface, his voice was rough as sand. ''Think about it, sugar. Whoever did this to him would love to play the same game with you. Take a good look, and ask yourself if that's how you want to end up.''

He waited a moment, then accepted her silence as understanding. ''Now you can go in the back room and save your sensibilities, or you can help me sort through this mess.''

When she turned, he assumed she'd walk away. That she might keep on walking, no matter the neighborhood. But she stopped at a file cabinet, grabbed a handful of papers. ''What am I looking for?''

''Anything.''

"That narrows it down. And why should there be anything left? They've already been here."

"He'd keep a backup somewhere." Jack hissed at the snowfall of papers. "Why the hell didn't he use a computer like a normal person?"

Rising, he went to the desk, wrenched out a drawer. He searched it, turning it over, checking the underside, the back, then tossing it aside and yanking out another. On the third try, he found a false back.

His quick grunt of approval had M.J. turning, watching him take out a penknife and pry at wood. Giving up her own search, she walked to him. By tacit agreement with him, she gripped the loosened edge and tugged while he worked the knife around. Wood splintered from wood.

"It's practically cemented on," Jack muttered. "And recently."

"How do you know it's recent?"

"It's clean. No dust, no grime. Watch your fingers. Here, you take the knife. Let me..." They switched jobs. He skinned his knuckles, swore, and continued to peel the wood back. All at once it popped free.

Jack took the knife again, cut through the tape affixing a key to the back of the drawer. "Storage locker," he muttered. "I wonder what Ralph has tucked away."

"Bus station? Train station? Airport?" M.J. leaned closer to study the key. "It doesn't have a name, just a number."

"I'd go with one of the first two. Ralph didn't like to fly, and the airport's a trek from here."

"That still leaves a lot of locks on a lot of boxes," she reminded him.

"We'll track it down."

"Do you know how many storage lockers there must be in the metropolitan area?"

He turned the key between his fingers and smiled thinly. "We only need one." He took her hand, and before she realized his intent, he'd cuffed them together again.

"Oh, for God's sake, Jack."

"Just covering my bases. Come on, we've got work to do."

At the first bus station, he'd grudgingly removed the cuffs before dragging M.J. into a phone booth, and making an anonymous call to the police to report the murder. Then he carefully wiped down the phone. "If they've got caller ID," he told her, "they'll track down where the call was made."

"And I take it your prints are on file."

He flashed a grin. "Just a little disagreement over pool in my misspent youth. Fifty dollars and time served."

Because he'd shifted, she was backed into the corner of the booth, pressed to the wall by his body. "It's a little crowded in here."

"I noticed." He lifted a hand, skimmed back the hair at her temple. "You did all right back there. A lot of women would have gotten hysterical."

"I don't get hysterical."

"No, you don't. So give me a break here, will

you?'' He tipped her face up, lowered his head. ''Just for a minute.'' And he closed his mouth over hers.

She could have resisted. She meant to. But it was an easy kiss, with need just a whispering note. It was almost friendly, could have been friendly, if not for the press of his body to hers, and the heat rising from it.

And an easy, almost friendly kiss shouldn't have made her want to cling, to hold on and hold tight. She compromised by fisting a hand on his back, not holding but not protesting.

If her lips softened under his, warmed and parted, it was only for a moment. It meant nothing. Could mean nothing.

''I want you.'' He murmured the words against her mouth, then again when his lips pressed to her throat. ''This is a hell of a time for it, a hell of a place. But I want you, M.J. I'm having a hard time getting past that.''

''I don't go to bed with strangers.''

''Who's asking you to?'' He lifted his head, met her eyes. ''We've got each other figured, don't we? And you're not the kind of woman who needs fussy dates or fancy words.''

''Maybe not.'' The fire he'd kindled inside her was still smoldering. ''Maybe I haven't figured out what I need.''

''Then think about it.'' He backed off, then took her hand and pulled her out of the booth. ''We'll check the lockers. Maybe we'll get lucky.''

They didn't. Not in that terminal or in the next

two. It was nearly one in the morning before he pocketed the key.

"I want a drink."

She let out a breath, rolled her shoulders. After twelve hours in a waking nightmare, she could see his point. "I wouldn't turn one down. You buying?"

"Why not?"

He steered clear of any of the places where he might be recognized and chose instead a dingy little dive not far from Union Station.

"Good thing I've had my shots." M.J. wrinkled her nose at the sticky, stamp-size table and checked the chair before she sat.

"It was either this or a fern bar. We can check out Union Station when we've had a break. Two of what you've got on tap," he told the waitress, and cracked a peanut.

"I don't know how places like this stay in business." With a critical eye, M.J. studied the atmosphere. Smoke-choked air, a generally stale smell, sticky floor littered with peanut shells, cigarette butts and worse. "A few gallons of disinfectant, some decent lighting, and this joint would turn up one full notch."

"I don't think the clientele cares." He glanced toward the surly-faced man at the bar, and the weary-eyed working girl who was casing him. "Some people just come into a bar to engage in the serious business of drinking until they're drunk enough to forget why they came into the bar to begin with."

She acknowledged his comment with a nod.

"That's the type I don't want in my place. You get them from time to time, but they rarely come back. They're not looking for conversation and music or a companionable drink with a pal. That's what I serve at my place."

"Like father, like daughter."

"You could say that." M.J.'s eyes narrowed in disapproval as the waitress slammed down their mugs. Beer sloshed over the tops. "She wouldn't last five minutes at M.J.'s."

"Rude barmaids have their own charm." Jack picked up his beer and sipped gratefully. "I meant what I said earlier." He grinned when her gaze narrowed on his. "About that, too, but I meant how you handled yourself. It was a tough room, M.J., for anybody."

"It was a first for me." She cleared her throat, drank. "You?"

"Yeah, and I don't mind saying I hope it's my last. Ralph was a jerk, but he didn't deserve that. I'd have to say whoever did that to him enjoyed his work. You've got some real bad people interested in you."

"It looks that way." And those same people, she thought, would be interested in Bailey and Grace. "How long do you figure it'll take to find the lock that fits that key?"

"No telling. Knowing Ralph, he wouldn't go too far afield. He hid the key in his office, not his apartment, so odds are the box is close."

But if it wasn't, it could be hours, even days, before they found it. She wasn't willing to wait that long. She took another gulp of beer. "I need the rest room." When he narrowed his eyes, she smirked. "Want to come with me?"

He studied her a moment, then moved his shoulders. "Make it fast."

She didn't rush toward the back, but her mind was racing. Ten minutes, she calculated. That was all she needed, to get out, get to the phone booth she'd seen outside and get through to Bailey.

She closed the door of the ladies' room at her back, scanned the woman in black spandex primping in the mirror, then grinned at the small casement window set high in the wall.

"Hey, give me a leg up."

The woman perfected a second coat of bloodred lipstick. "A what?"

"Come on, be a pal." M.J. hooked a hand on the narrow sill. "Give me a boost, will you?"

Taking her maddening time, the woman slid the top back on her tube of lipstick. "Bad date?"

"The worst."

"I know the feeling." She tottered over on icepick heels. "Do you really think you can squeeze through that? You're skinny, but it'll be a tight fit."

"I'll make it."

The woman shrugged, exuded a puff of too-sweet designer-knockoff perfume and cupped her hands. "Whatever you say."

M.J. bounced a foot in the makeshift stirrup, then boosted herself up until she had her arms hooked on the sill. A quick wriggle and she was chest-high. "Just another little push."

"No problem." Getting into the spirit, the woman set both hands on M.J.'s bottom and shoved. "Sorry," she said when M.J. cracked her head on the window and swore.

"It's okay. Thanks." She wiggled, grunted, twisted and forced herself through the opening. Head, then shoulders. Taking a quick breath, trying not to imagine herself remaining corked in the window, she muscled her way through with only a quick rip of denim.

"Good for you, honey."

M.J. stayed on her hands and knees long enough to shoot her assistant a quick grin. Then she was off and running. She dug in her pocket as she went for the quarter habitually carried there.

She could hear her mother's voice. *Never leave the house without money for a phone call in your pocket. You never know when you'll need it.*

"Thanks, Ma," she murmured, and reached the phone booth at a dead run. "Be there, be there," she whispered, plugging in the coin, stabbing numbers.

She heard Bailey's calm, cool voice answer on the second ring and swore as she recognized the recorded message.

"Where are you, where are you?" She clamped down on panic, took a breath. "Bailey, listen up," she began, the instant after the beep. "I don't know what the hell's going on, but we're in trouble. Don't stay there, he may come back. I'm in a phone booth outside some dive near—''

''Damn idiot.'' Jack reached in, grabbed her arm.

''Hands off, you son of a bitch. Bailey—'' But he'd already disconnected her. Using the confines of the booth to his advantage, he twisted her around and clamped the cuffs on so that her arms were secured. Then he simply lifted her up and tossed her over his shoulder.

He let her rant, let her kick, and had her dumped back into the car before a single Good Samaritan could take interest. Her threats and promises bounced off him as he peeled away from the curb and shot down side streets.

''So much for trust.'' And where there wasn't trust, he thought, there had to be proof. Cautious, he doubled back, scouting the area until he found a narrow alley half a block from the phone booth. He backed in, shut off the lights and engine.

Reaching over, he vised a hand around the back of her neck, pulled her face close. ''You want to see where your phone call would have gotten us? Just sit tight.''

''Take your hands off me.''

''At the moment, having my hands on you is the least of my concerns. Just be quiet. And wait for it.''

When his grip loosened, she jerked back. ''Wait for what?''

''It shouldn't take much longer.'' And, brooding into the dark, he watched the street.

It took less than five minutes. By his count, a little

more than fifteen since her call. The van crept up to the curb. Two men got out.

"Recognize them?"

Of course she did. She'd seen them only that morning. One of them had broken in her door. The other had shot at her. With a quick tremor of reaction, she shut her eyes. They'd traced the call from Bailey's line, she realized. Traced it quickly and efficiently.

And if Jack hadn't moved fast, they might very well have snapped her up just as quickly, just as efficiently.

The smaller of the two went into the bar while the other stood by the phone booth, scanning the street, one hand resting under his suit jacket.

"He'll pass the bartender a couple of bucks to see if you were in there, if you were alone, how long ago you left. They won't hang around long. They'll find out you're still with me, so they'll be looking for the car. We won't be able to use it anymore around here tonight."

She said nothing as the second man came back out, joined the first. They appeared to discuss something, argue briefly, and then they climbed back in the van. This time it didn't creep down the street, it rocketed.

She remained silent for another moment, continued to stare straight ahead. "You were right," she said at length. "I'm sorry."

"Excuse me? I'm not sure I heard that."

"You were right." She had to swallow when she

found herself distressingly close to tears. "I'm sorry."

Hearing the tears in her voice only heightened his temper. "Save it," he snapped, and started the engine. "Next time you want to commit suicide, just make sure I'm out of range."

"I needed to try. I couldn't not try. I thought you were overreacting, or just pushing my buttons. I was wrong. How many times do you want me to say it?"

"I haven't decided. If you start sniveling, I'm really going to get ticked."

"I don't snivel." But she wanted to. The tears were burning her throat. It cost nearly as much to swallow them as it would have to let them free.

She worked on calming herself as he drove out of the city and headed down a deserted back road in Virginia. The city lights giving way to comforting dark.

"No one's following us," she said.

"That's because I'm good, not because you're not stupid."

"Get off my back."

"If I'd sat in there another five minutes waiting for you, I could be as dead as Ralph right now. So consider yourself lucky I don't just dump you on the side of the road and take myself off to Mexico."

"Why don't you?"

"I've got an investment." He caught the look, the glimmer of wet eyes, and ground his teeth. "Don't look at me like that. It really makes me mad."

Swearing, he swerved to the shoulder. Yanking the

key from his pocket, he unlocked her hands, then slammed out of the car to pace.

Why the hell was he tangled up with this woman? he asked himself. Why hadn't he cut himself loose? Why wasn't he cutting loose right now? Mexico wasn't such a bad place. He could get himself a nice spot on the beach, soak up the sun and wait for all this to blow over.

Nothing was stopping him.

Then she got out of the car, spoke quietly. "My friend's in trouble."

"I don't give a damn about your friend." He whirled toward her. "I give a damn about me. And maybe I give one about you, though God knows why, because you've been nothing but grief ever since I watched you swagger up those apartment steps."

"I'll sleep with you."

That cut his minor tirade off in midstream. "What?"

She squared her shoulders. "I'll sleep with you. I'll do whatever you want, if you help me."

He stared at her, at the way the moonlight showered over her hair, at the way her eyes continued to glisten. And wanted her mindlessly.

But not in a barter.

"Oh, that's nice." Bitterness spewed through his voice. "That's great. I don't even have to tie you to the damn railroad tracks." He stepped toward her, grabbed her by the arms and shook. "What the hell do you take me for?"

"I don't know."

"I don't use women," he said between his teeth. "And when I take one to bed, it's a two-way street. So thanks for the offer, but I'm not interested in the supreme sacrifice."

He let her go, started back to the car. Fury had him turning back. "Do you think your friend would appreciate the gesture if he found out you'd slept with me to help him?"

She took a deep, steadying breath. The depth of his sense of insult had gone farther toward gaining her trust than any promise or oath could have. "No. It wouldn't stop me, but no."

She stepped toward him, stopping only when they were within an armspan. "My friend's name is Bailey James. She's a gemologist."

He recognized the name from the doctored paperwork. But the pronoun was the most vital piece of information to him. "She?"

"Yes, she. We went to college together, we roomed together. One of the reasons I located in D.C. was because of Bailey, and Grace. She was our other roommate. They're the closest friends I have, ever have had. I'm afraid for them, and I need your help."

"Bailey's the one who sent you the stone?"

"Yes, and she wouldn't have done it without good reason. I think she may have sent the third one to Grace. It would be Bailey's kind of logic. She does a lot of consulting work for the Smithsonian."

Suddenly tired, M.J. rubbed her gritty eyes. "I haven't seen her since Wednesday evening. We were supposed to get together tonight at the pub. I put a note under her door to check the time with her. I work a lot of nights, she works days, so even though we live right across the hall from each other, we pass a lot of notes under the door. And lately, since she got the job working on the Three Stars for the Smithsonian, she's been putting in a lot of overtime. I didn't think anything of it when I didn't see her for a couple days.''

"And Friday you got the package."

"Yes. I called her at work right away, but I only got the service. They'd closed until Tuesday. I'd forgotten she'd told me they were closing down for the long weekend, but that she'd probably work through it. I went by, but the place was locked up. I called Grace, got her machine. By that time, I was annoyed with both of them. I figured I just was going to have to assume Bailey had her reasons and would let me know. So I went to work. I just went on to work.''

"There's no use beating yourself up about that. You didn't have much choice."

"I have a key to her place. I could have used it. We've got this privacy arrangement, which is why we pass notes. I didn't use the key out of habit.'' She shuddered out a breath. "But she didn't answer the phone now, when I called from outside that bar, and it was two o'clock in the morning. Bailey's arrow-straight, she's not out at 2:00 a.m., but she didn't answer the phone. And I'm afraid... What they did to that man... I'm afraid for her.''

He put his hands on her shoulders, and this time they were gentle. "There's only one thing to do.''

Because he thought she might need it, he pressed a kiss to her brow. "We'll check it out."

She let out her breath on a shuddering sigh. "Thanks."

"But this time you have to trust me."

"This time I will."

He opened the door, waited for her to get in. "The other friend you were talking about, the he?"

She pushed her hair back, looked up. "There is no he."

So he leaned down, captured her mouth with his in one long, searing kiss. "There's going to be."

He took a chance, went back to Union Station first. They'd be looking for his car, true enough, but he was banking on the moldy gray of the Olds, with its scarred vinyl top, blending in.

And he intended to be quick.

Bus and train stations were all very much the same in the middle of the night, he thought. The people curled in chairs or stretched out in blankets weren't all waiting for transportation. Some of them just had nowhere else to go.

"Keep moving," he told M.J. "And keep sharp. I don't want to get cornered in here."

She wondered, as she matched her pace to his, why such places smelled of despair in the early hours. There was none of the excitement, the bustle, the anticipation of goings and comings, so evident during the daylight hours. Those who traveled at night, or looked for a dry corner to sleep, were usually running low on hope.

"You said we were going to check on Bailey."

"Soon as I'm done with this." He headed straight for the storage lockers, did a quick scan. "Sometimes you just get lucky," he murmured, and, matching numbers, slid the key into a lock.

M.J. leaned over his shoulders. "What's in there?"

"Stop breathing down my neck and I'll see. Backup copies of your paperwork," he said, and handed them to her. "Souvenir for you."

"Gee, thanks. I'm really going to want a memento of our little vacation jaunt." But she stuffed them in her bag after a cursory glance. Her interest perked up when Jack drew out a small notebook covered in fake black leather. "That looks more promising."

"Where's his running money?" Jack wondered, deeply disappointed not to find any cash when he swiped his hand around the locker a last time. "He'd have kept some ready in here if he had to catch a train fast."

"Maybe he'd already taken it out."

He opened his mouth to disagree, then shut it again. "Yeah, you've got a point. Could be he wanted to have it on him if he wanted to make a fast exit." Brows knit, he flipped through the book. "Names, numbers."

"Addresses? Phone numbers?" she asked, craning her neck to try to see.

"No. Amounts, dates. Payoffs," he decided.

"Looks to me like Ralph was running a little blackmail racket on the side."

"Salt of the earth, your friend Ralph."

"Former friend," Jack said automatically, before he remembered it was literally true. "Very former," he murmured. "If this got out, he'd have lost more than his business. He'd have been doing time in a cell."

"Do you think someone decided to blackmail the blackmailer?"

"Follows. And not everybody puts the arm on for money." He shook his head. According to the figures, Ralph had made more than a decent income with his sideline. "Sometimes they go for blood."

"What good does this do us?" M.J. demanded.

"Not a hell of a lot." He tucked the book into his back pocket, scanned the terminal again. "But someone Ralph was squeezing squeezed back. Or, more likely, someone who knew about Ralph's little moonlighting project saved the information until it became useful."

"Then killed him," M.J. added as her stomach tightened. "Whoever did isn't just connected with that little book, or Ralph. They're connected to Bailey through the stones. I have to find her."

"Next stop," he said, and took her hand in his.

Chapter 6

M.J. understood the risk, and prepared herself to make no arguments whatever about Jack's instructions. She'd ask no questions. This was his area of expertise, after all, and she needed a pro.

That vow lasted less than thirty minutes.

"Why are you just driving around?" she demanded. "You should have turned left back at the corner. Did you forget how to get there?"

"No, I didn't forget how to get there. I don't forget how to get anywhere."

She rolled her eyes in his direction. "Well, if you've got a map in your head, you've just taken a wrong turn."

"No, I didn't."

Men, she thought on a huff of breath. "I'm telling

you—I live here. The apartment's three blocks that way."

He'd told himself he'd be patient with her. She was under a lot of stress, they'd both put in a long, rough day.

His good intentions fled to the place M.J.'s vow had gone.

"I know where you live," he snapped. "I had your place staked out for two hours while you were out shopping."

"I wasn't shopping. I was buying, and that's entirely different. And you still haven't answered my very simple question."

"Do you ever shut up?"

"Are you ever anything but rude?"

He braked at a light, drummed his fingers on the wheel. "You want to know why I'm driving around, I'll tell you why I'm driving around. Because there are two guys with guns in a van looking for us, specifically in this car, and if they happen to be in the area, I'd just as soon see them before they see us. And the reason for that is, I'd prefer not being shot tonight. Is that clear enough?"

She folded her arms over her chest. "Why didn't you just say so in the first place?"

His answer was a mutter as he turned again. He drove sedately for a half block, then pulled over to the curb, shut off the engine.

"Why are you stopping here? We're still blocks away. Look, Jack, if your testosterone's low and you're lost, I won't hold it against you. I can—"

"I'm not lost." He put both hands in his hair, and was tempted to pull. "I never get lost. I know what I'm doing." He reached over, popped open the glove box.

"Well, then, why—"

"We're going on foot," he told her, and grabbed a pencil-beam flashlight and a .38. He made sure she saw the gun and took his time checking the clip. She barely blinked at it.

"That doesn't make any sense. If we have to—"

"We're doing this my way."

"Oh, big surprise. I'm simply asking—"

"I'm tired of answering, *really* tired of answering." But he sighed out a breath. "We're going to cut down this street, then between those two yards, around the building on the next block, then through to the back of the apartment. We're going on foot because we'll be tougher to spot if they've got your building staked out."

She thought it over, considered the angles, then nodded. "Well, that makes sense."

"Thanks, thanks a lot." He grabbed her purse and, while she stuttered out a shocked protest, emptied her wallet of cash.

"Just what the hell do you think you're doing? That's my money." She snatched back her empty wallet as he stuffed bills in his pocket, then goggled as he plucked out the diamond and pushed it in after the bills. "Give me that. Are you out of your mind?"

She made a grab for him. Jack simply shoved her back against the seat, held her in place and, risking another bloody lip, crushed his mouth to hers. She wriggled, muttered what he assumed were oaths, popped her fist against his ribs. Then she decided to cooperate.

And her cooperation, hot, avid, was a great deal more difficult to resist than her protests. He lost himself in her for a moment, experienced the shock of being helpless to do otherwise.

It was like the first time. Consuming. The thought circled in his mind that he'd been waiting all his life to find his mouth pressed to hers.

Just that simple. Just that terrifying.

The fist she'd struck him with relaxed, and her open fingers slid around, up his back, hooked possessively over his shoulder. Mine, she thought.

Just that easy. Just that staggering.

When he shifted back, they stared at each other in the dim light, two strong-minded people who'd just had their worlds tilt under them. Her hand was still gripped on his shoulder, and his on hers.

"Why'd you do that?" she managed.

"It was mostly to shut you up." His hand skimmed up her shoulder, into her hair. "It changed."

Very slowly, she nodded. "Yes, it did."

He had a strong urge to drag her into the back seat and play teenager. The idea nearly made him smile. "I can't think about this now."

"No, me either."

The hand in her hair moved and, in a surprisingly

sweet gesture took hers, laced fingers with hers. "We're going to do more than think about it later."

"Yeah." Her lips curved a little. "I guess we are."

"Let's go. No, don't take the purse." When she opened her mouth to argue, he simply tugged it away from her, tossed it into the back. "M.J., that thing weighs a ton. We may have to move fast. I'm taking the cash, and the stone, because they might make the car, or we may not get back to it."

"All right." She got out, waited for him on the sidewalk. Glanced briefly at the gun he secured in a shoulder holster. "I know this is risky. I have to do it, Jack."

He took her hand again. "Then let's do it."

They followed the route he'd mapped out, slipped between yards, a dog barking halfheartedly at them. The moon was out, a bright beacon that both guided their path and spotlighted them.

He had a moment to intensely wish he'd had her change out of the white T-shirt. It glowed in the dark like a lit-up flag. But she moved well, with quiet, long strides. He already knew she could run if necessary. He had to be satisfied with that.

"You have to do what I tell you," he began, keeping his voice low as he surveyed the back of her building. "I know that goes against the grain for you, but you'll have to swallow it. If I tell you to move, you move. If I tell you to run, you run. No questions, no arguments."

"I'm not stupid. I just like to know the reasons."

"This time you just do what you're told, and we'll discuss my reasoning later."

She struggled to fall into step. "Her car's here," she told him quietly. "The little white compact."

"Okay, so maybe she's home." Or, he thought, she hasn't been able to drive. But he didn't think that was what M.J. needed to hear. "We'll go in the side, through the fire door, work our way around to the stairs. No noise, M.J., no conversation."

"Okay."

Her eyes were already on Bailey's windows as they hurried toward the side door. The windows were dark, the curtains drawn. Bailey left her curtains open, was all she could think. Bailey liked to look out the windows and rarely shut out her view.

They slipped inside like shadows and, with Jack a half step in the lead, walked quietly to the steps. The security light beamed, lighting the hall and stairs. Jack glanced out the front door, keeping well to the side. If anyone was watching, he mused, they'd be spotted easily going into the light.

It was a chance they'd have to take.

As they moved up the stairs, he listened for any sound, any movement. It was so late it was early. The building slept. There wasn't even the murmur of a late-night TV behind any of the doors they passed on the second floor.

When they reached the third, M.J. made her first sound, just a quickly indrawn breath, instantly muffled. There was police tape over her door.

"Your neighbor with the bunny slippers called the

cops,'' Jack murmured. ''Odds are they're looking for you, too.'' He held out a hand. ''Key?''

She turned, kept her eyes on Bailey's door as she dug into her pocket, handed it to him. He gestured her back toward the steps to give her room to run away, unsheathed his gun, then unlocked the door.

Keeping low, he used his light to scan, saw no movement. Holding a hand up to keep M.J. in place, he stepped inside. What he'd seen had already decided him that no one was there, but he wanted to check the bedroom, the kitchen, before M.J. joined him.

He'd taken the first steps when her gasp, unmuffled this time, had him turning. ''Stay back,'' he ordered. ''Stay quiet.''

''Oh, God. Bailey.'' She shot toward the bedroom, leaping over ripped cushions, overturned chairs like a hurdler coming off the mark.

He reached the door a step ahead, shoved her roughly out of the way. ''Hold it together, damn it,'' He hissed, then opened the door. ''She's not here,'' he said a moment later. ''Go close the front door, lock it.''

On legs that trembled, she crossed back, taking a winding path through the destruction of the living room. She closed the door, locked it, then leaned back weakly.

''What have they done to her, Jack? Oh, God, what have they done to her?''

''Sit down. Let me look.''

She squeezed her eyes tight, fought for control.

Images flitted through her head. Her and Grace sitting in the shade of a boulder while Bailey gleefully hunted rocks. The three of them giggling like fools late at night over jug wine. Bailey, a wave of blond hair falling into her face soberly contemplating a pair of Italian shoes in a store display.

"I'll help," she said, and let out a whoosh of breath. "I can help."

Yeah, he thought, watching the way her spine stiffened, her shoulders squared, she probably could. "Okay, you've got to keep it quiet, and keep it quick. We can't risk the lights, or much time."

He skimmed the beam over the room. Contents of drawers and closets had been tossed and scattered. A few breakables smashed. The cushions, the mattress, even the back of chairs, had been slashed so that stuffing poured out in an avalanche of destruction.

"You're not going to be able to tell if anything's missing in all this mess." He surveyed the surface damage and calculated that the woman had gone in for tchotchkes in a big way. "But I can tell you, I don't think your friend was here when this went on."

M.J. pressed a hand to her heart, as though to hold in hope. "Why?"

"This wasn't a struggle, M.J. It was a search, a quick, messy and mostly quiet one. I'd say we have a pretty good idea what they were looking for. Whether they found it or not—"

"She'd have it with her," M.J. said quickly. "Her note was very clear that I should keep the stone with me. She'd have kept it with her."

"If that's true, then odds are she still has it. She wasn't here," he repeated, scanning the light into the living room. "She didn't put up a fight here, she wasn't hurt here. There's no blood."

Her knees wobbled again. "No blood." And she pressed a hand to her mouth to cut off the little sob of relief. "Okay. She's okay. She went underground, the same way we did."

"If she's as smart as you say she is, that's just what she'd do."

"She's smart enough to run if she had to run." It helped to look at the tumbled room with a more careful eye. "She doesn't have her car, so she's on foot or using public transportation." And M.J.'s heart sank at the thought of it. "She doesn't know the streets, Jack. She doesn't know the ropes. Bailey's brilliant, but she's naive. She trusts too easily, likes to believe the best in people. She's sweet," M.J. added, on a little shudder.

"She must have picked up something from you." He appreciated the fact that she could smile at that, even a little. "Let's just take a quick look through this stuff, see if anything pops out. Check her clothes—you could probably tell if she'd packed things."

"She has a travel kit, fully stocked. She'd never go anywhere without it." Buffered by that simple, everyday fact, M.J. headed into the bath to check the narrow linen closet.

Even there, items had been pulled out, the shelves stripped, bottles opened and emptied. But she found the kit itself, opened and empty on the floor, recognized several of its contents—the travel toothbrush, the fold-up hair brush, the travel-size shampoos and soaps.

"It's here." She stepped into the bedroom, did her best to inventory clothes. "I don't think she took anything. There's a suit missing. It's fairly new, so I remember. A neat little blue silk. She might be wearing it. Hell, shoes and bags, I don't know. She collects them like stamps."

"She keep a stash anywhere?"

Insulted, she jerked up her head. "Bailey doesn't do drugs."

"Not drugs." Patience, he told himself, and cast his eyes at the ceiling. "You sure have an opinion of me, sugar. Money, cash."

"Oh." She rose from her crouch. "Sorry. Yeah, she keeps some cash." It bothered her a little, but she led him into the kitchen. "Boy, is she going to hate seeing this. She really likes things ordered. It's kind of an obsession with her. And her kitchen." She kicked some cans, coated with the flour and sugar and coffee that had been dumped out of canisters. "You'd be hard-pressed to find a crumb in the toaster."

"I'd say we've all got bigger problems than housekeeping."

"Right." She bent down, retrieved a soup can. "It's one of those fake safe things," she explained, and twisted off the top. "She didn't take her emergency money, either." And there was relief in that.

"She probably hasn't even been back here since— Hey!" She jerked the can back, but he'd already scooped out the cash. "Put that back."

"Listen, we can't risk using plastic, so we need money. Cash money." He stuck a comfortingly thick wad of it in his pocket. "You can pay her back."

"I can? You took it."

"Details," he muttered, grabbing her hand. "Let's go. There's nothing here, and we're pushing our luck."

"I could leave her a note, in case she comes back. Stop dragging me."

"She may not be the only one who comes back." He yanked her through the door and kept tugging until they were heading down the stairs.

"I've got to see about Grace."

"One friend at a time, M.J. We're getting out of Dodge for a while."

"I could call her, on my phone, or your cellular. Jack, if Bailey and I are in the middle of this, Grace is, too."

"Travel as a pack, do you?"

"So?" She hurried toward the side door with him, fueled by fresh worry. "I have to contact her. She has a place in Potomac. I don't think she's there. I think she's up at her country place, but—"

"Quiet." He eased open the door, scanned the quiet side lot, the sleeping neighborhood. It had been smooth and easy so far. Smooth and easy made him edgy. "Keep it down until we're clear, will you? God, you've got a mouth."

She snarled with it as he pulled her outside and started eating up the ground. "I don't see what the problem is. Whoever was looking for Bailey and the diamond have been and gone."

"Doesn't mean they won't come back." He caught the glint of moonlight off the chrome of the van just as it squealed into the lot. "Sometimes I hate being right. Go!" he shouted, shoving her ahead of him.

He whirled to protect her back, tried a quick prayer that they hadn't been spotted. And decided God was busy at the moment, when the van doors burst open. The gun was in his hand, the first shot fired, before he spun around and sprinted after her.

He hoped the single shot would give his pursuers something to consider. "I said go!" he snapped out when he all but mowed her down.

"I heard a shot. I thought—"

"Don't think. Run." He grabbed her hand to be certain she did, and was grateful she had no problem keeping pace.

They stormed between the yards, and this time the dog took a keener interest, sending up a wild din that carried for blocks. Moonlight flowed in front of them. Though he heard no footsteps pounding in pursuit, Jack didn't break stride as they whipped around the side of a building, turned the corner.

He took time to scan the street, then hit the ground running. "In" was all he said as he sprinted to the driver's side.

He needn't have bothered with the order. M.J. was

already wrenching open the door and diving onto the seat. "They didn't come after us," she panted. "That's bad. They should have come after us."

"You catch on." He flicked the key, hit the gas and shot out from the curb just as the van screamed around the corner. "Grab on to something."

Though she wouldn't have believed it possible, he spun the big car into a fast U-turn, riding two wheels over the opposing curb. His bumper kissed lightly off the fender of a sedan, and then he was screaming down the quiet suburban street at sixty.

He took the first turn with the van three lengths behind. "You know how to use a gun?"

M.J. picked it up off the seat. "Yeah."

"Let's hope you don't have to. Get your seat belt on, if you can manage it," he suggested as he jerked the Olds around another corner. M.J.'s elbow rapped against the dash. "And don't point that thing in this direction."

"I know how to handle a gun." Teeth set, she braced herself and watched through the rear window. "Just drive. They're closing in."

Jack flicked his gaze into the rear view, measured the distance from the oncoming headlights. "Not this time," he promised.

He wound through the streets like a snake, tapping the brake, flooring the gas, whipping the wheel so that his tires whined. The challenge of it, the speed, the insanity, had him grinning.

"I like to do this to music." And he switched the radio up to blare.

"You're crazy." But she found herself grinning madly back at him. "They want to kill us."

"People in hell want snow cones." He hit a four-lane and pushed the car to eighty. "This tank might not look like much, but she moves."

"So does that van. You're not shaking them."

"I haven't gotten started." He skimmed his gaze fast, left, right, then plowed recklessly through a red light. Traffic was sparse, even as they zipped toward downtown. "That's the trouble with D.C.," he commented. "No nightlife. Politicians and ambassadors."

"It has dignity."

"Yeah, right." He wrestled the car around a curve at fifty, and began to travel the rabbit warren of narrow back streets and circles. He heard the ping of metal against metal as a bullet hit his rear fender.

"Now they're getting nasty."

"I think they're trying to shoot out the tires."

"I just bought these babies."

Old or new, she thought, if a bullet hit rubber, the game was over. M.J. took a deep breath, held it, then popped out the window to her waist and fired.

"Are you crazy?" His heart jumped into his throat and nearly had him crashing into a lamppost. "Get your head back in here before you get it blown off."

Grim-eyed, too wired to be afraid, she fired again. "Two can play." With the third shot, she hit a headlight. The shattering glass pumped her adrenaline. It hardly mattered that she'd been aiming at the windshield. "I hit them."

With a mindless snarl, Jack grabbed the seat of her jeans and dragged her in. For the first time in his life, his hands trembled on the wheel of his car. "Who do you think you are, Bonnie Parker?"

"They backed off."

"No, they didn't. I'm outrunning them. Just let me handle this, will you?"

He twisted his way back to the four-lane, careened straight across, shooting over the median with a bone-rattling series of bumps. Sparks spewed out like stars as steel skidded on concrete. With a skill M.J. admired, he wrestled the car into a wide arc, then headed north.

"They're trying it." She twisted in the seat, poked her head out the window again, despite Jack's steady swearing. "I don't think they're gonna—" She hooted at the sound of crunching metal. "They're backing up, heading north on the southbound."

"I can see. I don't need a damn play-by-play. Get back in here. Strap in this time."

He hit the on-ramp for the Beltway at sixty. And had gained just enough time, he calculated, to make it work. He barreled off at the first exit and headed into Maryland.

"You lost them." She crawled over and gave him an enthusiastic smack on the cheek. "You're good, Dakota."

"Damn right." He was also shaky. The moment he felt he could afford it, he pulled to the shoulder and wiped her grin away by grabbing her shoulders and giving her a hard, teeth-rattling shake. "Don't you ever do anything so stupid again. You're lucky you didn't fall out of the window, or get your head shot off.''

''Cut it out, Jack.'' Her hand was already fisting. ''I mean it.'' Then she went limp as he hauled her against him and held tight. His face was buried in her hair, his heart was pounding. ''Hey.'' Baffled, moved, she patted his back. ''I was just pulling my weight.''

''Don't.'' His mouth found hers in a desperate kiss. ''Just don't.'' And as abruptly as he'd grabbed her, he shoved her away. ''You've gotten to me,'' he muttered, furious at the emotions storming through him. ''Just shut up.'' His head whipped around when she opened her mouth. ''Just shut up. I don't want to talk about it.''

''Fine.'' Her own stomach was trembling. As if the fate of the world depended on it, she meticulously buckled her seat belt as he pulled back onto the road. ''I'd really like to call my friend Grace.''

His hands were tensed on the wheel, but he kept his voice even. ''We can't risk it now. We don't know what kind of equipment they've got in that van, and they're too close yet. We'll see what we can manage tomorrow.''

Knowing she'd have to settle for that, she rubbed her restless hands on her knees. ''Jack, I know what you risked going to Bailey's to try to ease my mind. I appreciate it.''

''Just part of the service.''

''Is it?''

He glanced over, met her eyes. "Hell, no. I said I don't want to talk about it."

"I'm not talking about it." She wasn't sure she knew how, or what to do about these unexpected feelings swimming through her. "I'm thanking you."

"Then you're welcome. Look, I'm heading back to the Bates Motel. Which are you more—hungry or tired?"

That, at least, didn't take any thought. "Hungry."

"Good, so am I."

She had a lot of considering to do, M.J. decided. Her friend was missing, she had a priceless blue diamond in her possession—or in Jack's pocket—and she'd been chased, shot at and handcuffed.

Added to that, she was very much afraid she was falling for some tough-eyed, swaggering bounty hunter who drove like a maniac and kissed like a dream.

A hot, sweaty dream.

And she knew barely more of him than his name.

It made no sense, and though she enjoyed being reckless in some areas, her heart wasn't one of them. She'd always kept a firm hand there, and it was frightening to feel that grip slipping over a man she'd literally rammed into only the day before.

She wasn't a romantic woman, or a fanciful one. But she was an honest woman. Honest enough to admit that whatever danger she was facing from the outside, she was facing danger just as great, just as real, from her own heart.

* * *

He was trembling with fury. Incompetence. It was unacceptable to find himself surrounded by utter incompetence. It was true he'd had to hire the men quickly, and with only the thinnest of recommendations, but their failure to execute one small task, to deal with one woman, was simply outrageous.

He had no doubt he could have dealt with her handily himself, if he could have risked the exposure.

Now, with the moon set and the stars fading, he stood on the terrace, calming his soul with a glass of wine the color of new blood.

It was partly his fault, he conceded. Certainly, he should have checked more carefully into the matter of Jack Dakota. But time had been of the essence, and he had assumed the fool of a bail bondsman was capable of following the orders to assign someone just competent enough to take her, and wise enough to turn her over.

Apparently, Jack Dakota wasn't a wise man, but a stubborn one. And the woman was infuriatingly lucky. M. J. O'Leary. Well, perhaps she had the luck of the Irish, but luck could change.

He would see to that.

Just as he would see to Bailey James. She would have to surface eventually. He'd be ready. And Grace Fontaine... Pity.

Well, he would find the third stone, as well.

He would have all of them. And a heavy price would be paid by all who had tried to stop him.

His fingers snapped the fragile stem. Glass tinkled

on the stone. Wine splattered and pooled. Grimly he smiled down, watched the red liquid seek the cracks.

More than blood would be spilled, he promised himself.

And soon.

Chapter 7

They settled in the little all-night diner just down from the motel. Coffee, strong enough to walk on, came first, served by a sleepy-eyed waitress wearing a cotton-candy-pink uniform and a plastic name tag that declared her Midge.

M.J. shifted in the booth, catching her jeans on the torn vinyl of the seat, perused the hand-typed menu under its plastic coating, then propped an elbow on the scarred surface of the coffee-stained linoleum that covered their table.

A very ancient country-and-western tune was twanging away on the juke, and the air was redolent of the thick odor of frying grease.

Aesthetics weren't served there, but breakfast was. Twenty-four hours a day.

"That's almost too perfect," M.J. commented after she ordered a whopping breakfast, including a short stack, eggs over and a rasher of bacon. "She even looks like a Midge—hardworking, competent and friendly. I always wondered if people grew into their names or vice versa. Like Bailey—cool, studious, smart. Or Grace, elegant, feminine and generous."

Jack rubbed a hand over the stubble on his chin. "So what's M.J. stand for?"

"Nothing."

He cocked a brow. "Sure it does. Mary Jo, Melissa Jane, Margaret Joan, what?"

She sipped her coffee. "It's just initials. And that's been made legal, too."

His lips curved. "I'll get you drunk and you'll spill it."

"Dakota, I come from a long line of Irish pub owners. Getting me drunk is beyond your capabilities."

"We'll have to check that out—maybe in your place. Dark wood?" he asked with a half smile. "Lots of brass. Irish music, live on weekends?"

"Yep. And not a fern in sight."

"Now we're talking. And seeing as you own it, you can buy the first round as soon as we're clear."

"It's a date." She picked up her cup again. "And, boy, am I looking forward to it."

"What, we're not having fun yet?"

She eased back as the waitress set their heaping plates on the table. "Thanks." Then picked up a fork and dug in. "It's had its moments," she told him. "Can I see Ralph's book?"

"What for?"

"So I can admire its handsome plastic binding," she said sweetly.

"Sure, why not?" He lifted his hips, drew it out and tossed it on the table. As she flipped through the pages, he sampled his eggs. "See anyone you know?"

It was the cocky tone of his voice that made her delighted to be able to glance up at him, smile and say, "Actually, I do."

"What?" He would have snatched the book back if she hadn't held it out of reach. "Who?"

"T. Salvini. That's got to be one of Bailey's stepbrothers."

"No kidding?"

"No kidding. There's a five and three zeros after his name. Just think. Tim or Tom did business with Ralph. You did business with Ralph, now I'm—in a loose manner of speaking—doing business with you." Those dark-river-green eyes shifted up, met his. "Small world, right, Jack?"

"From where I'm sitting," he agreed.

"Here's another payment, about five K. Looks like the bill came in on the eighteenth of the month— goes four, no, five months back." Thoughtfully she tapped the book on the edge of the table. "Now I wonder what one, or both, of the creeps did that was worth twenty-five thousand to keep Ralph quiet about it."

"People do things all the time they want kept quiet—and they pay for it, one way or another."

She angled her head. "You're a real student of human nature, aren't you, Dakota? And a cynic, as well."

"Life's a cynical journey. Well, we've got one solid connection back to Ralph. Maybe we'll pay the creeps a visit soon."

"They're businessmen," she pointed out. "Slimy, from my viewpoint, but murder's a big jump. I can't see it."

"Sometimes it's a much smaller step than you'd think." He took the book back, pocketed it again. "On that cynical journey."

"I can see them cooking the books," she said speculatively. "Timothy has a gambling problem—meaning he likes to play and tends to lose."

"Is that so? Well, Ralph had a lot of connections when it came to, let's say, games of chance. That's a link that slides neat onto the chain."

"So Ralph finds out the creep's playing deep, maybe skimming the till to keep from getting his legs broken, and he puts the pressure on."

"It might work. And Salvini whines to somebody who's got more muscle—somebody who wants the Stars." He moved his shoulders and decided to give it a chance to brew. "In any case, that wasn't bad work, sugar."

"It was great work," she corrected.

"I'll cop to good. And you looked pretty natural with your hips hanging out the car window, shooting at a speeding van." He drowned his pancakes in syrup. "Even if it did stop my heart. If you ever decide to change careers, you'd make a passable skip tracer."

"Really?" She wasn't sure if she should be complimented or worried by the assessment. She decided to be flattered. "I don't think I could spend my life on the hunt—or being hunted." She shook enough salt on her eggs to make Jack—a sodium fan—wince. "How do you? Why do you?"

"How's your blood pressure?"

"Hmm?"

"Never mind. I figure you go with your strengths. I'm good at tracking, backtracking, then figuring out the steps people are planning to take. And I like the hunt." He grinned wolfishly. "I love the hunt. Doesn't matter what size the prey is, as long as you bring them down."

"Crime's crime?"

"Not exactly. That's a cop attitude. But if you've got the right point of view, it's just as satisfying to snag some deadbeat father running from back child support as it is to bag a guy who shot his business partner. You can bring down both if you get to know your quarry. Mostly they're stupid—they've got habits they don't break."

"Such as?"

"A guy dips into the till where he works. He gets caught, charged, then he jumps bail. Odds are he's got friends, relatives, a lover. It won't take long before he asks somebody for help. Most people aren't loners. They think they are, but they're not. Something always pulls them back. They'll make a call, a visit. Leave a paper trail. Take you.''

Surprised, she frowned. "I hadn't done anything."

''That's not the issue. You're a smart woman, a self-starter, but you wouldn't have gone far, you wouldn't have gone long without calling your friends.'' He scooped up eggs, smiled at her. ''In fact, that's just what you did.''

''And what about you? Who would you call?''

''Nobody.'' His smile faded. He continued to eat as the waitress topped off their coffee.

''No family?''

''No.'' He picked up a slice of bacon, snapped it in two. ''My father took off when I was twelve. My mother handled it by hating the world. I had an older brother, signed with the army the day he hit eighteen. He decided not to come back. I haven't heard from him in ten, twelve years. Once I got into college, my mother figured her job was done and hit the road. You could say we don't keep in touch.''

''I'm sorry.''

He jerked his shoulder against the sympathy, irritated with himself for telling her. He didn't talk family. Ever. With anyone.

''You haven't seen your family in all these years,'' she continued, unable to prevent herself from probing just a bit. ''You don't know where they are—they don't know where you are?''

''We weren't what you'd call close, and we didn't

spend enough time together to be considered dys-
functional."

"But still—"

"I always figured it was in the blood," he said,
cutting her off. "Some people just don't stay put."

All right, she thought, his family was out of the
conversation. It was a tender spot, even if he didn't
realize it. "What about you, Jack? How long have
you stayed put?"

"That's part of the appeal of the job. You never
know where it's going to take you."

"That's not what I meant." She searched his face.
"But you knew that."

"I never had any reason to stay." Her hand rested
on the table, an inch from his. He was tempted to
take it, just hold it. That worried him. "I know people, a lot of people. But I don't have friends—not
the way you do with Bailey and Grace. A lot of us
go through life without that, M.J."

"I know. But do you want to?"

"I never gave it a hell of a lot of thought." He
rubbed both hands over his face. "God, I must be
tired. Philosophizing over breakfast in the Twilight
Diner at five in the morning."

She glanced out the window at the lightening sky
to the east, the all-but-empty road. "'And down the
long and silent street, the dawn—'"

"'With silver-sandaled feet, crept like a frightened
girl.'" Finishing the quote, he shrugged. She was
goggling at him.

PLAY "LUCKY 7" AND GET
FIVE FREE GIFTS!

HOW TO PLAY:

1. With a coin, carefully scratch off the silver box at the right. Then check the claim char to see what we have for you—**FREE BOOKS** and a gift—**ALL YOURS! ALL FREE!**

2. Send back this card and you'll receive brand-new Silhouette Intimate Moments® novel These books have a cover price of $4.50 each, but they are yours to keep absolutely free

3. There's no catch. You're under no obligation to buy anything. We charge nothing— ZERO—for your first shipment And you don't have to make any minimum number of purchases—not even one!

4. The fact is thousands of readers enjoy receiving books by mail from the Silhouette Reader Service™ months before they're available in stores. They like the convenience of home delivery and they love our discount prices!

5. We hope that after receiving your free books you'll want to remain a subscriber. But the choice is yours—to continue or cancel, any time at all! So why not take us up on ou invitation, with no risk of any kind. You'll be glad you did!

YOURS FREE!

This lovely necklace will add glamour to your most elegant outfit! Its cobra-link chain is a generous 18" long, and its lustrous simulated cultured pearl is mounted in an attractive pendant! Best of all, it's ABSOLUTELY FREE, just for accepting our NO-RISK offer.

NOT ACTUAL SIZE

PLAY THE

LUCKY
SLOT
MACHINE
GAME!

Just scratch off the silver box with a coin. Then check below to see the gifts you get!

YES!

I have scratched off the silver box. Please send me all the gifts for which I qualify. I understand I am under no obligation to purchase any books, as explained on the back and on the opposite page.

345 CIS CDVF
(C-SIL-IM-12/97)

Name _____

Address _____ Apt.# _____

City _____ Prov. _____ Postal Code ____

WORTH FOUR FREE BOOKS PLUS A FREE SIMULATED PEARL DROP NECKLACE!

WORTH THREE FREE BOOKS!

WORTH TWO FREE BOOKS!

WORTH ONE FREE BOOK!

The Silhouette Reader Service™ — Here's how it works

Accepting free books places you under no obligation to buy anything. You may keep the books and gift and return the shipping statement marked "cancel." If you do not cancel, about a month later we'll send you 6 additional novels, and bill you just $3.71 each, plus 25¢ delivery per book and GST. * That's the complete price—and compared to cover prices of $4.50 each—quite a bargain! You may cancel at any time, but if you choose to continue, every month we'll send you 6 more books, which you may either purchase at the discount price...or return to us and cancel your subscription.

*Terms and prices subject to change without notice.
Canadian residents will be charged applicable provincial taxes and GST.

01956119199-L2A5X3-BR01

SILHOUETTE READER SERVICE
PO BOX 609
FORT ERIE ON   L2A 9Z9

MAIL ➤ POSTE
Canada Post Corporation/Société canadienne des postes

Postage paid   **Port payé**
If mailed in Canada   si posté au Canada

Business   **Réponse**
Reply   **d'affaires**

01956119199   01

"How do you know that? Just what did you take in college?"

"Whatever appealed to me."

Now she grinned, propped her elbows on the table. "Me too. I drove my counselors crazy. I can't tell you how many times I was told I had no focus."

"But you can quote Oscar Wilde at 5:00 a.m. You can shoot a .38, drop-kick your average man, you eat like a trucker, understand ancient Roman gods, and I bet you mix a hell of a boilermaker."

"The best in town. So here we are, Jack, a couple of people most would say are overeducated for their career choices, drinking coffee at an ungodly hour of the morning, while a couple of guys in a van with one headlight hunt for us and the pretty rock you've got in your pocket. It's the Fourth of July, we've known each other less than twenty-four hours under very possibly the worst of circumstances, and the person who brought us together is dead as Moses."

She pushed her plate aside. "What do we do now?"

He took bills out of his pocket, tossed them on the table. "We go to bed."

The motel room was still tacky, cramped and dim. The thin flowered spread was still mussed where they had stretched out on it hours before.

Only hours, she thought. It felt like days. A lifetime. More than a lifetime. It felt as if she'd known him forever, she realized as she watched him empty his pocket onto the dresser, that he'd been a vital part of her forever.

If that wasn't enough, maybe the wanting was. Maybe wanting like this was the best thing to hold on to when your world had gone insane. There was nothing and no one left to trust but him.

Why should she say no? Why should she turn away from comfort, from passion? From life?

Why should she turn away from him, when every instinct told her he needed those things as much as she did?

He turned, and waited. He could have seduced her. He had no doubt of it. She was running on sheer nerves now, whether she knew it or not. So she was vulnerable, and needy, and he was there.

Sometimes that alone was enough.

He could have seduced her, would have, if it hadn't been important. If she hadn't been so inexplicably and vitally important. Sex would have been a relief, a release, a basic physical act between two free-willed adults.

And that should have been all he wanted.

But he wanted more.

He stayed where he was, beside the dresser, as she stood at the foot of the bed.

"I've got something to say," he began.

"Okay."

"I'm in this with you until it's over because that's the way I want it. I finish what I start. So I don't want anything that comes from gratitude or obligation."

If her heart hadn't been jumping, she might have smiled. "I see. So if I suggested you sleep in the bathtub, that wouldn't be a problem?"

He eased a hip onto the dresser. "It'd be your problem. If that's what you want, you can sleep in the bathtub."

"Well, you never claimed to be a gentleman."

"No, but I'll keep my hands off you."

She angled her head, studied him. He looked dangerous, plenty dangerous, she decided as her pulse quickened. The dark stubble, the wild mane of hair, those hard gray eyes so intense in that tough, rawboned face.

He thought he was giving her a choice.

She wondered if either of them was fool enough to believe she had one.

So her smile was slow, arrogant. She kept her eyes on his as she reached down, tugged her T-shirt out of her jeans. She watched his gaze flick down to her hands, follow them up as she pulled the shirt over her head, tossed it aside.

"I'd like to see you try," she murmured, and unsnapped her jeans. He straightened on legs gone watery when she began to lower the zipper.

"I want to do that."

With heat already tingling in her fingertips, she let her hands fall to her sides. "Help yourself."

Her shoulders were long, fascinating curves. Her breasts were pale and small and would cup easily in a man's palm. But for now, he looked only at her face.

He took his time, tried to, crossing to her, catching the metal tab between his thumb and finger, drawing it slowly down. And his eyes were on hers when he slid his hand past the parted denim and cupped her.

Felt her, hot, naked. Felt her tremble, quick, deep.

"I had a feeling."

She let out a careful breath, drew in another through lungs that had become stuffed with cotton. "I didn't get to my laundry this week."

"Good." He eased the denim down another inch, slid his hands around her bottom. "You're built for speed, M.J. That's good, because this isn't going to be slow. I don't think I could manage slow right now." He yanked her against him, arousal to arousal. "You're just going to have to keep up."

Her eyes glinted into his, her chin angled in a dare. "I haven't had any trouble keeping up with you so far."

"So far," he agreed, and ripped a gasp from her when he lifted her off her feet and clamped his hungry mouth to her breast.

The shock was stunning, glorious, an electric sizzle that snapped through her blood and slapped her heartbeat into overdrive. She let her head fall back and wrapped her legs tight around his waist to let him feed. The scrape of his beard against her skin, the nip of teeth, the slide of his tongue—each a separate, staggering thrill.

And each separate, staggering thrill tore through her system and left her quivering for more.

The fall to the bed—a reckless dive from a cliff.

The grip of his hands on hers—another link in the chain. His mouth, desperate on hers—a demand with only one answer.

She pulled at his shirt, rolled with him until he was free of it and they were both bare to the waist. And found the muscles and bones and scars of a warrior's body. The heat of flesh on flesh raged through her like a firestorm.

Her hands and mouth were no less impatient than his. Her needs no less brutal.

With something between an oath and a prayer, he flipped her over, dragging at her jeans. His mouth busily scorched a path down her body as he worked the snug denim off. Desire was blinding him with hammer blows that stole the breath and battered the senses. No hunger had ever been so acute, so edgy and keen, as this for her. He only knew if he didn't have her, all of her, he'd die from the wanting.

Those long naked limbs, the energy pulsing in every pore, those harsh, panting gasps of her breath, had the blood searing through his veins to burn his heart. Wild for her, he yanked her hips high and used his mouth on her.

The climax screamed through her, one long, hot wave with jagged edges that had her sobbing out in shock and delight. Her nails scraped heedlessly down his back, then up again until they were buried in his thick mane of gold-tipped hair. She let him destroy her, welcomed it. And, with her body still shuddering from the onslaught, wrestled him onto his back to tear at the rest of his clothes.

She felt his heart thud, could all but hear it. Their flesh, slick with sweat, slid smoothly as they grappled. His fingers found her, pierced her, drove her past desperation. If speech had been possible, she would have begged.

Rather than beg, she clamped her thighs around him, and took him inside, fast and deep.

His fingers dug hard into her hips when she closed over him. His breath was gone; his heart stopped. For an instant, with her raised above him, her head thrown back, his hands sliding sinuously up her body, he was helpless.

Hers.

Then she began to move, piston-quick, riding him ruthlessly in a wild race. Her breath was sobbing, her hands were clutched in her hair. In some part of his brain he realized that she, too, was helpless.

His.

He reared up, his mouth greedy on her breast, on her throat, wherever he could draw in the taste of her while they moved together in a merciless, driving rhythm.

Then he wrapped his arms around her, pressed his lips to her heart, groaning out her name as they shattered each other.

They stayed clutched, joined, shuddering. Time was lost to him. He felt her grip slacken, her hands slide weakly down his back, and brushed a kiss over her shoulder. He lay back, drawing her with him so that she was sprawled over his chest.

He stroked a hand over her hair and murmured, "It's been an interesting day."

She managed a weak chuckle. "All in all." They were sticky, exhausted, and quite possibly insane, she thought. Certainly, it was insane to feel this happy, this perfect, when everything around you was wrecked.

She could have told him she'd never been intimate with a man so quickly. Or that she'd never felt so in tune, so close to anyone, as with him.

But there didn't seem to be a point. What was happening to them was simply happening. Opening her eyes, she studied the stone resting atop the scarred dresser. Did it glow? she wondered. Or was it simply a trick of the light of the room?

What power did it have, really, beyond material wealth? It was just carbon, after all, with some elements mixed in to give it that rare, rich color. It grew in the earth, was of the earth, and had once been taken, by human hands, from it.

And had once been held in the hands of a god.

The second stone was knowledge, she thought, and closed her eyes. Perhaps some things were known only to the heart.

"You need to sleep," Jack said quietly. The tone of his voice made her wonder where his mind had wandered.

"Maybe." She rolled off him, stretched out on her stomach across the width of the bed. "My body's tired, but I can't shut off my head." She chuckled again. "Or I can't now that I'm able to think again. Making love with you is a regular brain drain."

"That's a hell of a compliment." He sat up, running a hand over her shoulder, down her back, then stopping short at the subtle curve of her bottom. Intrigued, he narrowed his eyes, leaned closer. Then grinned. "Nice tattoo, sugar."

She smiled into the hot, rumpled bedspread. "Thanks. I like it." She winced when he switched on the bedside lamp. "Hey! Lights out."

"Just want a clear look." Amused, he rubbed his thumb over the colorful figure on her butt. "A griffin."

"Good eye."

"Symbol of strength—and vigilance."

She turned her head, cocked it so that she could see his face. "You know the oddest things, Jack. But yeah, that's why I chose it. Grace got this inspiration about the three of us getting tattoos to celebrate graduation. We took a weekend in New York and each got our little butt picture."

Her smile slid away as thoughts of her friends weighed on her heart. "It was a hell of a weekend. We made Bailey go first, so she wouldn't chicken out. She picked a unicorn. That's so like her. Oh, God."

"Come on, turn it off." He was mortally afraid she might weep. "As far as we know, she's fine. No use borrowing trouble," he continued, kneading the muscles of her back. "We've got plenty of our own.

In a couple hours, we'll clean up, go out and cruise around, try to call Grace.''

"Okay." She pulled in the emotion, tucked it into a corner. "Maybe—''

"Did you run track in college?''

"Huh?''

The sudden change of subject accomplished just what he'd wanted it to. It distracted her from worry. "Did you run track? You've got the build for it, and the speed.''

"Yeah, actually, I was a miler. I never liked relays. I'm not much of a team player.''

"A miler, huh?'' He rolled her over and, smiling, traced a fingertip over the curve of her breast. "You gotta have endurance.''

Her brows lifted into her choppy bangs. "That's true.''

"Stamina.'' He straddled her.

"Absolutely.''

He lowered his head, toyed with her lips. "And you have to know how to pace yourself, so you've got wind for that final kick.''

"You bet.''

"That's handy.'' He bit her earlobe. "Because I'm planning on pacing myself this time. You know the saying, M.J.? The one about slow and steady winning the race?''

"I think I've heard of it.''

"Why don't we test it out?'' he suggested, and captured her mouth with his.

* * *

This time she slept, as he'd hoped she would. Facedown again, he mused, studying her, crossways over the bed. He stroked her hair. He couldn't seem to touch her enough, and couldn't remember ever having this need to touch before. Just a brush on the shoulder, the link of fingers.

He was afraid it was ridiculously sentimental, and was grateful she was asleep.

A man with a reputation for being tough and cynical didn't care to be observed mooning like a puppy over a sleeping woman.

He wanted to make love with her again. That, at least, was understandable. To lose himself in sex— the hot, sweaty kind, or the slow and sweet kind.

She'd turn to him, he knew, if he asked. He could wake her now, arouse her before her mind cleared. She'd open for him, take him in, ride with him.

But she needed to sleep.

There were shadows under her eyes—those dark, witchy green eyes. And when the flush of passion faded from her skin, her cheeks had been pale with fatigue. Sharp-boned cheeks, defined by a curve of silky skin.

He pressed his fingers to his eyes. Listen to him, he thought. The next thing he knew, he'd be composing odes or something equally mortifying.

So he nudged her over, made himself comfortable. He'd sleep for an hour, he thought, setting his internal clock. Then they would step back into reality.

He closed his eyes, shut down.

* * *

M.J. woke to the sound of rain. It reminded her of lazy mornings, summer showers. Snuggling into the pillow, shifting from dream to dream.

She did so now, sliding back into sleep.

The horse leaped over the narrow stream, where shallow water flashed blue. Her heart leaped with it, and she clutched the man tighter. Smelled leather and sweat.

Around them, buttes rose like pale soldiers into a sky fired by a huge white sun. The heat was immense.

He was in black, but it wasn't her knight. The face was the same—Jack's face—but it was shadowed under a wide-brimmed black hat. A gun belt rode low on his hips, instead of a silver sword.

The empty land stretched before them, wide as the sea, with waves of rocks, sharp-edged as honed knives. One misstep, and the ground would be stained with their blood.

But he rode fearlessly on, and she felt nothing but the power and excitement of the speed.

When he reined in, turned in the saddle, she poured herself into his arms, met those hard, demanding lips eagerly with her own.

She offered him the stone that beat with light and a fire as blue as the hottest flame.

"It belongs with the others. Love needs knowledge, and both need generosity."

He took it from her, secured it in the pocket over his heart. "One finds the other. Both find the third." His eyes lit. "And you belong to me."

In the shadow of a rock, the snake uncoiled, hissed out its warning. Struck.

M.J. shot up in bed, a scream strangled in her throat. Both hands pressed to her racing heart. She swayed, still caught in the dream fall.

The snake, she thought with a shudder. A snake with the eyes of a man.

Lord. She concentrated on steadying her breathing, controlling the tremors, and wondered why her dreams were suddenly so clear, so real and so odd.

Rather than stretch out again, she found a T-shirt—Jack's—and slipped it on. Her mind was still fuzzy, so it took her a moment to realize it wasn't rain she was hearing, but the shower.

And that alone—knowing he was just on the other side of the door—chased away the last remnants of fear.

She might be a woman whose pride was based on being able to handle herself in any situation. But she'd never faced one quite like this. It helped to know there was someone who would stand with her.

And he would. She smiled and rubbed the sleep out of her eyes. He wouldn't back down, he wouldn't turn away. He would stick. And he would face with her whatever beasts were in the brush, whatever snakes there were in the shadows.

She rose, raking both hands through her hair, just as the bathroom door opened.

He stepped out, a billow of steam following. A dingy white towel was hooked at his waist, and his body still gleamed with droplets of water. His hair was slick and wet to his shoulders, gold glinting through rich brown.

He had yet to shave.

She stood, heavy-eyed, tousled from sleep, wearing nothing but his wrinkled T-shirt, tattered at the hem that skimmed her thighs.

For a moment, neither of them could do more than stare.

It was there, as real and alive in the tatty little room as the two of them. And it gleamed as bright, as vital, as the stone that had brought them to this point.

Jack shook his head as if coming out of a dream—perhaps one as vivid and unnerving as the one M.J. had awakened from. His eyes went dark with annoyance.

"This is stupid."

If she'd had pockets, her hands would have been in them. Instead, she folded her arms and frowned back at him. "Yeah, it is."

"I wasn't looking for this."

"You think I was?"

He might have smiled at the insulted tone of her voice, but he was too busy scowling, and trying desperately to backpedal from what had just hit him square in the heart. "It was just a damn job."

"Nobody's asking you to make it any different."

Eyes narrowed, he took a step forward, challenge in every movement. "Well, it is different."

"Yeah." She lowered her hands to her sides, lifted her chin. "So what are you going to do about it?"

"I'll figure it out." He paced to the dresser, picked up the stone, set it down again. "I thought it was just the circumstances, but it's not." He turned, studied her face. "It would have happened anyway."

Her heartbeat was slowing, thickening. "Feels like that to me."

"Okay." He nodded, planted his feet. "You say it first."

"Uh-uh." For the first time since he'd opened the door, her lips twitched. "You."

"Damn it." He dragged a hand through his dripping hair, felt a hundred times a fool. "Okay, okay," he muttered, though she was waiting silently, patiently. Nerves drummed under his skin, his muscles coiled like wires, but he looked her dead in the eye.

"I love you."

Her response was a burst of laughter that had him clamping his teeth until a muscle jerked in his jaw. "If you think you're going to play me for a sucker on this, sugar, think again."

"Sorry." She snorted back another laugh. "You just looked so pained and ticked off. The romance of it's still pittering around in my heart."

"What, do you want me to sing it?"

"Maybe later." She laughed again, the delighted sound rolling out of her and filling the room. "Right now I'll let you off the hook. I love you right back. Is that better?"

The ice in his stomach thawed, then heated into a warm glow. "You could try to be more serious about it. I don't think it's a laughing matter."

"Look at us." She pressed a hand to her mouth and sat down on the foot of the bed. "If this isn't a laughing matter, I don't know what is."

She had him there. In fact, he realized, she had him, period. Now his lips curved, with determination. "Okay, sugar, I'm just going to have to wipe that smirk off your face."

"Let's see if a big tough guy like you can manage it."

She was grinning like a fool when he shoved her back on the bed and rolled on top of her.

Chapter 8

She had to learn to defer to him on certain matters, M.J. told herself. That was compromise, that was relationship. The fact was, he had more experience in situations like the one they were in than she did. She was a reasonable person, she thought, one who could take instruction and advice.

Like hell she was.

"Come on, Jack, do I have to wait till you drive to Outer Mongolia to make one stupid phone call?"

He flipped her a look. He'd been driving for exactly ten minutes. He was surprised she'd waited that long to complain. She was worried, he reminded himself. The past twenty-four hours had been rough on her. He was going to be reasonable.

In a pig's eye.

''You use that phone before I say, and I'll toss it out the window.''

She drummed her fingers on the little pocket phone in her hand. ''Just answer me this. How is anybody going to trace us through this portable? We're out in the middle of nowhere.''

''We're less than an hour outside of D.C., city girl. And you'd be surprised what can be traced.''

Okay, maybe he wasn't exactly sure himself if it could be done. But he thought it was possible. If her friend's phone was tapped, and whoever was after them had the technology, it seemed possible that the frequency of her flip phone could be a trail of sorts.

He didn't want to leave a trail.

''How?''

He'd been afraid she'd ask. ''Look, that thing's essentially a radio, right?''

''Yeah, so?''

''Radios have frequencies. You tune in on a frequency, don't you?'' It was the best he could do, and it was a relief to see her purse her lips and consider it. ''Plus, I want to put some distance between where we are and where we're staying. If it was the FBI on our tails, I'd want them chasing in circles.''

''What would the FBI want with us?''

''It's an example.'' He didn't beat his head on the steering wheel, but he wanted to. ''Just deal with it, M.J. Just deal with it.''

She was trying to, trying to remind herself that it had only been a day, after all. One single day.

But her life had changed in that single day.

"At least you could tell me where we're going."

"I'm taking 15, north toward Pennsylvania."

"Pennsylvania?"

"Then you can make you call. After, we'll head southeast, toward Baltimore." He flicked her another glance. "If the Os are in town, we can take in a game."

"You want to go to a ball game?"

"Hey, it's the Fourth of July. Ball games, beer, parades and fireworks. Some things are sacred."

"I'm a Yankee fan."

"You would be. But the point is, a ballpark's a good place to lose ourselves for a couple hours—and a good place for a meet if you're able to contact Grace."

"Grace at a baseball game?" She snorted. "Right."

"It's a good cover," he began, then frowned. "Your friend has something against the national pastime?"

"Sports aren't exactly Grace's milieu. Now, a nice, rousing fashion show, or maybe a thrilling opera."

It was his turn to snort. "And you're friends?"

"Hey, I've been known to go to the opera."

"In chains?"

She had to laugh. "Practically. Yeah, we're friends." She let out a sigh. "I guess it's hard, surface-wise, to see why. The scholar, the Mick and the princess. But we just clicked."

"Tell me about them. Start with Bailey, since this starts with Bailey."

"All right." She drew a deep breath, watched the scenery roll by. Little snatches of country, thick with trees and hills that rolled. "She's lovely, has this fragile look about her. Blond, brown-eyed, with rose-petal skin. She has a weakness for pretty things, silly, pretty things, like elephants. She collects them. I gave her one carved out of soapstone for her birthday last month."

Remembering how normal it had all been, how simple, had her pressing her lips together. "She likes old movies, especially the film noir type, and she can be a little dreamy at times. But she's very focused. Of the three of us back in college, she was the only one who knew exactly what she wanted and worked toward it."

He liked the sound of Bailey, Jack thought. "And what did she want?"

"Gemology. She's fascinated by rocks, stones. Not just jewel types. We keep talking about the three of us going to Paris for a couple weeks, but last year we ended up in Arizona, rockhounding. She was happy as a pig in slop. And she's had a lot of unhappiness in her life. Her father died when she was a kid. He was an antique dealer—so that's another of her weaknesses, beautiful old things. Anyway, she adored her dad. Her mother tried to hold the business together, but it must have been rough. They lived up in Connecticut. You can still hear New England in her voice. It's classy."

She lapsed into silence a moment, struggling to push back the worry. "Her mother married again a few years later, sold the business, relocated in D.C. Bailey was fond of the guy. He treated her well, got her interested in gems—that was his area—sent her to college. Her mother died when she was in college—a car accident. It was a rough time for Bailey. Her stepfather died a couple years later."

"It's tough, losing people right and left."

"Yeah." She glanced at Jack, thought of him losing father, brother, mother. Perhaps never really having them to lose. "I've really never lost anyone."

He understood where her mind had gone, and he shrugged. "You get through. You go on. Didn't Bailey?"

"Yeah, but it scarred her. It's got to scar a person, Jack."

"People live with scars."

He wouldn't discuss it, she realized, and turned back to the scenery. "Her stepfather left her a percentage of the business. Which didn't sit well with the creeps."

"Ah, yeah, the creeps."

"Thomas and Timothy Salvini—they're twins, by the way, mirror images. Slick-looking characters in expensive suits, with hundred-dollar haircuts."

"That's one reason to dislike them," Jack noted. "But it's not your main one."

"Nope. I never liked their attitudes—toward Bailey, and women in general. It's easiest to say Bailey considered them family from the get-go, and the sentiment wasn't returned. Timothy was particularly rough on her. I get the impression they mostly ignored her before their old man died, and then went ballistic when she inherited part of Salvini in the will.''

"And what's Salvini?''

"That's their name, and the name of the gem business. They design, buy, sell gems and jewelry out of a fancy place in Chevy Chase.''

"Salvini... Can't say I've heard of it, but then I don't buy a lot of baubles.''

"They sell some awesome glitters—especially the ones Bailey designs. And they do consultant work for estates, museums. That's primarily Bailey's forte, too. Though she loves design work.''

"If Bailey does design work and consulting, what do the creeps do?''

"Thomas handles the business end—accounts, sales, takes a lot of trips to check out sources for gems. Timothy works in the lab when it suits him, and likes to stride around the showroom looking important.''

Restless, she reached out to fiddle with the buttons of his stereo and had her fingers slapped. "Hands off.''

"Touchy about your toys, aren't you?'' she muttered. "Well, anyway, it's a pretty posh little firm, old established rep. It was her contacts at the Smithsonian that copped them the job with the Three Stars. She was dancing on the ceiling when it came through, couldn't wait to get her hands on them, put them under one of those machines she uses. The somethingmeters, and whattayascopes she uses in their lab.''

"So she was verifying authenticity, assessing value.''

"You got it. She was dying for us to see them, so Grace and I went in last week. That was the first time I'd laid eyes on them—but they seemed almost familiar. Spectacular, almost unreal, yet familiar. I suppose it's because Bailey'd described them to us.'' She rolled her shoulders to toss off the sensation, and the memory of the dreams. "You've seen the one, touched it. It's magnificent. But to see the three of them, together, it just stops your heart.''

"Sounds to me as though they stopped someone's conscience. If Bailey's as honest as you say—''

M.J. interrupted him. "She is.''

"Then we'll have to check out the stepbrothers.''

Her brows shot up. "Would they actually have the nerve to try to steal the Three Stars?'' she wondered. "Could that be why Ralph was blackmailing one of them, rather than the gambling?''

"No.''

"Well, why not?'' Then she shook her head, answering her own question. "Couldn't be—the payments started months ago, and they'd just recently got the contract.''

"There you go.''

She brooded over it a moment longer. "But maybe they were planning to steal the Stars. If they were trying to pull a fast one, got away with it, it would destroy their business...the business their father slaved a lifetime to build," she added slowly. "And that would destroy Bailey. Even the thought of it. She'd do almost anything to prevent that from happening."

"Like ship off the stones to the two people in the world she felt she could trust without question."

"Yeah—and face down her stepbrothers. Alone." Fear was a claw in her throat. "Jack."

"Stay logical." His voice snapped to combat the waver in hers. "If they're involved in this—and I'd say it fits—it means they've got a client, a buyer. And they need all three Stars. She's safe as long as they don't. She's safe as long as we're out of reach."

"They'd be desperate. They could be holding her somewhere. They might have hurt her."

"Hurt's a long way from dead. They'd need her alive, M.J., until they round up all three. And from the rundown you've just given me, your pal may have a fragile side, and she may be naive, but she's not a chump."

"No, she's not." Steadying herself, M.J. looked at the phone in her lap. The call, she realized, wasn't just a risk for herself, but a risk for all of them. "If you want to drive to New York before I use this, it's okay with me."

He reached out, squeezed a hand over hers. "We're not going to Yankee Stadium, no matter how much you beg."

"I don't just owe you for me now. I should have

realized it before. I owe you for Bailey, and for Grace. I've put them in your hands, Jack.''

He drew his away, clamped it on the wheel. "Don't get sloppy on me, sugar. It pisses me off.''

"I love you.''

His heart did a long, slow circle in his chest, made him sigh. "Hell. I guess you want me to say it again, now.''

"I guess I do.''

"I love you. What's the M.J. stand for?''

It made her smile, as he'd hoped it would. "Look, Jack, wild sex and declarations of love are one thing. But I haven't known you long enough for that one.''

"Martha Jane. I really think it's Martha Jane.''

She made a rude buzzing sound. "Wrong. And that puts you out of this round, sir, better luck next time.''

There'd be a birth certificate somewhere, he mused. He knew how to hunt. "Okay, tell me about Grace.''

"Grace is a complicated woman. She's utterly, unbelievably beautiful. That's not an exaggeration. I've seen grown men turn into stuttering fools after one flash of her baby blues.''

"I'm looking forward to meeting her.''

"You'll probably swallow your tongue, but that's all right, I'm not the jealous sort. And it's kind of a kick to watch guys go into instant meltdown around Grace. You flipped through the pictures in my wallet when you searched my purse, didn't you?''

"Yeah, I took a look.''

"There's a couple of me with Grace and Bailey in there."

He skimmed his mind back, focused in. And didn't want to tell her he'd barely noted the blonde or the brunette. The redhead had taken most of his attention. "The brunette—wearing a big silly hat in one of them."

"Yeah, that was on our rockhounding trip last year. We had a tourist snap it. Anyway, she's gorgeous, and she grew up privileged. And orphaned. She lost her folks young and lived with an aunt. The Fontaines are filthy rich."

"Fontaine...Fontaine..." His mind circled. "As in Fontaine Department Stores?"

"Right the first time. They're rich, stuffy, snotty snobs. Grace enjoys shocking them. She was expected to do her stint at Radcliffe, do the obligatory tour of Europe, and land the appropriate rich, stuffy, snotty snob husband. She's done everything but cooperate, and since she's got mountains of money of her own, she doesn't really give two damns what her family thinks."

She paused, considered. "I don't think she'd give two damns if she was flat broke, either. Money doesn't drive Grace. She enjoys it, spends it lavishly, but she doesn't respect it."

"People who work for their money respect it."

"She's not a do-nothing trust-funder." M.J. said, immediately defensive. "She just doesn't care if people see her that way. She does a lot of charity work—quietly. That's private. She's one of the most generous people I know. And she's loyal. She's also contrary and moody. She'll take off for days at a time when the whim strikes her. Just go. It might be Rome—or it might be Duluth. She just has to go. She has a place up in western Maryland—I guess you'd call it a country home, but it's small and sweet. Lots of land, very isolated. No phone, no neighbors. I think she was going there this weekend.''

She shut her eyes, tried to image. "I don't know if I could find the place. I've only been up there once, and Bailey did the driving. Once I get out of the city, all those country roads look the same. It's in the mountains, near some state forest.''

"It might be worth checking out. We'll see. Would she go to her family if there was trouble?''

"The last place.''

"How about a man?''

"Why would you depend on something you could twist into knots with a smile? No, there's no man she'd go to.''

He thought about that one awhile, then blinked, remembered and grinned. "Grace Fontaine—the Ivy League Miss April. It was the hat in the wallet shot that threw me off. I'd never forget that…face.''

"Really?'' Voice dry as dirt, she shifted to look at him over the top of her sunglasses. "Do you spend a lot of your time drooling over centerfolds, Dakota?''

"I did over Miss April,'' he admitted cheerfully, and rubbed a hand over his heart. "My God, you're pals with Miss April.''

"Her name's Grace, and she posed for that years ago, when we were in college. She did it to needle her family."

"Thank the Lord. I think I still have that issue somewhere. I'm going to have to take a much closer look now. What a body," he remembered, fondly. "Women built like that are a gift to mankind."

"Perhaps you'd like to pull over, and we'll have a moment of silence."

He looked over, kept right on grinning. "Gee, M.J., your eyes are greener. And you said you weren't the jealous sort."

"I'm not." Normally. "It's a matter of dignity. You're having some revolting, prurient fantasy about my best friend."

"It's not revolting, I promise. Prurient, maybe, but not revolting." He took the punch on the arm without complaint. "But it's you I love, sugar."

"Shut up."

"Do you think she'll sign the picture for me? Maybe right across the—"

"I'm warning you."

Fun was fun, he thought, but a man could push his luck. In more ways than one. He turned off 15, headed east.

"Wait, I thought we were going up to P.A. to call."

"You just said Grace had a place in western Maryland. It wouldn't be smart to head in that general direction just now. Change of plans. We head in toward Baltimore first. Go ahead and make the call. I think we've said our last goodbye to our little motel paradise." He smiled patted her hand. "Don't worry, sugar, we'll find another."

"It couldn't possibly be the same. I hope," she added, and dialed hurriedly. "It's ringing."

"Keep it short, don't say where you are. Just tell her to go to a public phone, public place, and call you back."

"I—" She swore. "It's her machine. I was afraid of this." She tapped her fist impatiently against her knees as Grace's recorded voice flowed through the receiver. "Grace, pick up, damn it. It's urgent. If you check in for messages, don't go home. Don't go to the house. Get to a public phone and call my portable. We're in trouble, serious trouble."

"Wrap it up, M.J."

"Oh, God. Grace, be careful. Call me." She disconnected with a little catch of breath. "She's up in the mountains—or she got a wild hair and decided to fly to London for the Fourth. Or she's on the beach in the West Indies. Or…they've already found her."

"Doesn't sound like a lady who's easy to track. I'm leaning toward your first choice." He cut off on the interstate, headed north. "We're going to circle around a little, then stop and fill up the tank. And buy a map. Let's see if we can jog some of your memory and find Grace's mountain hideaway."

The prospect settled her nerves. "Thanks."

"Isolated, huh?"

"It's stuck in the middle of the woods, and the woods are stuck in the middle of nowhere."

"Hmm. I don't suppose she walks around naked up there." He chuckled when she hit him. "Just a thought."

They found a gas station, and a map. In a truck stop just off the interstate, they stopped for lunch. With the map spread out over the table, they got down to business.

"Well, there's only, like, a half a dozen state forests in western Maryland," Jack commented, and forked up some of his meat-loaf special. "Any one of them ring a bell?"

"What's the difference? They're all trees."

"A real urbanite, aren't you?"

She shrugged, bit into her ham sandwich. "Aren't you?"

"Guess so. I never could understand why people want to live in the woods, or in the hills. I mean, where do they eat?"

"At home."

They looked at each other, shook their heads. "Most every night, too," he agreed. "And where do they go for fun, for a little after-work relaxation? On the patio. That's a scary thought."

"No people, no traffic, no restaurants or movie theaters. No life."

"I'm with you. Obviously our pal Grace isn't."

"*My* pal," she said with an arched brow. "She likes solitude. She gardens."

"What, like tomatoes?"

"Yeah, and flowers. The time we went up, she'd

been grubbing in the dirt, planting—I don't know, petunias or something. I like flowers, but all you have to do is buy them. Nobody says you have to grow them. There were deer in the woods. That was pretty cool," she remembered. "Bailey got into the whole business. It was okay for a couple days, but she doesn't even have a television up there."

"That's barbaric."

"You bet. She just listens to CDs and communes with nature or whatever. There's a little store—had to be at least four miles away. You can get bread and milk or sixpenny nails. It looked like something out of Mayberry, except that's in the South. There was a bank, I think, and a post office."

"What was the name of the town?"

"I don't know. Dogpatch?"

"Funny. Try to imagine the route, just more or less. You'd have headed up 270."

"Yeah, and then onto 70 near, what is it? Frederick. I zoned out some. Think I even slept. It's an endless drive."

"You had pit stops," he prompted her. "Girls don't take road trips without plenty of pit stops."

"Is that a slam?"

"No, it's a fact. Where'd you stop—what did you do?"

"Somewhere off 70. I was hungry. I wanted fast food."

She shut her eyes, tried to bring it back.

You're still eating like a teenager, M.J.

So?

Why don't we try a salad for a change?

Because a day without fries is a sad and wasted day.

It made her smile, remembering now how Bailey had rolled her eyes, laughed, then given in.

"Oh, wait. We grabbed a quick lunch, but then she saw this sign for antiques. Big antique barnlike place. She went orgasmic, had to check it out. It was off the interstate, had a silly country-type name. Ah…" She strained for it. "Rabbit Hutch, Chicken Coop. No, no, with water. Trout Stream. Beaver Creek!" she remembered. "We stopped to antique at this huge flea market or whatever it's called at Beaver Creek. She'd have spent the weekend there if I hadn't dragged her out. She bought this old bowl and pitcher for Grace—like a housewarming gift. I bought her a rocking chair for her porch. We had a hell of a time loading it in Bailey's car."

"Okay." With a nod, he folded the map. "We'll finish eating, then head toward Beaver Creek. Take it from there."

Later, when they stood in the parking lot of the antique mart, M.J. sipped a soft drink out of a can. She'd done the same on the trip with Bailey, and she hoped it would somehow jog her memory.

"I know we got back on 70. Bailey was chattering away about some glassware—Depression glass. She was going to come back and buy the place out. There was some table she wanted, too, and she was irritated she hadn't snapped it up and had it shipped. I won the tune toss."

"The what?"

"The tune toss. Bailey likes classical. You know, Beethoven. Whenever we drive, we flip a coin to see who gets to pick the tunes. I won, so we went for Aerosmith—my version of longhair."

"I think we're made for each other. It's getting scary." He leaned down, nipped her mouth with his. "What was she wearing?"

"What is this sudden obsession with how my friends dress?"

"Just bring it all back. Complete the picture. The more details, the clearer it should be."

"Oh, I get it." Mollified, she pursed her lips and studied the sky. "Slacks, sort of beige. Bailey shies away from bold colors. Grace is always giving her grief about it. A silk blouse, tailored, sort of pink and pale. She had on these great earrings. She'd made them. Big chunks of rose quartz. I tried them on while she was driving. They didn't suit me."

"Pink wouldn't, not with that hair."

"That's a myth. Redheads can wear pink. We got off the interstate onto a western route. I can't remember the number, Jack. Bailey had it in her head. It was written down, but she didn't need me to navigate."

He consulted the map. "68 heads west out of Hagerstown. Let's see if it looks familiar."

"I know it was another couple hours from here," she said as she climbed back in. "I could drive for a while."

"No, you couldn't."

She skimmed her gaze over the car, noting that the back door was hooked shut with wire. "This heap is hardly something to be proprietary about, Jack."

His jaw set. The heap had, until recently, been his one true love. "There's more chance of you remembering if we stick with the plan."

"Fine." She stretched out her legs as he turned out of the parking lot. "Do you ever think about a paint job?"

"The car has character just the way it is. And it's what's under the hood that counts, not a shiny surface."

"What's under the hood," she said, then glanced at the stereo system. "And in the dash. I bet that toy set you back four grand."

"I like music. What about that Tinkertoy you drive?"

"My MG is a classic."

"It's a kiddie car. You must have to fold up your legs just to get behind the wheel."

"At least when I parallel-park, it's not like docking a steamship in port."

"Pay attention to the road, will you?"

"I am." She offered him the rest of her soft drink. "I know it looks like it, but you don't actually live in this car, do you?"

"When I have to. Otherwise, I've got a place on Mass Avenue. A couple of rooms."

Dusty furniture, he thought now. Mountains of books, but no real soul. No roots, nothing he couldn't leave behind without a second thought.

Just like his life had been, up to the day before.

What the hell was he doing with her? he thought abruptly. There was nothing behind him that could remotely be called a foundation. Nothing to build on. Nothing to offer.

She had family, friends, a business she'd forged herself. What did they have in common, other than the situation they were in, similar tastes in music and a preference for city life?

And the fact that he was in love with her.

He glanced over at her. She was concentrating now, he noted. Leaning forward in the seat, frowning out the window as she tried to pick out landmarks.

She wasn't beautiful, he thought. He might have been blind in love, but he would never have termed her by so simple a term. That odd, foxy face caught the eye—certainly the male eye. It was sexy, unique, with the contrast of planes and angles and the curve of that overlush mouth.

Her body was built for speed and movement, rather than for fantasy. Yet he'd lost himself in it, in her.

He knew he'd turned a corner when he met her, but hadn't a clue where the road would lead either of them.

"This is the road." She turned, beamed at him, and stopped his heart. "I'm sure of it."

He bumped up the speed to sixty-five. As long as one of them was sure, he thought.

Chapter 9

The road cut straight through the mountain. M.J. supposed it was some sort of nifty feat of engineering, but it made her uneasy. Particularly all the signs warning of falling rock and those high, jagged walls of cliffs on either side of them.

Muggers she could understand, anticipate, but who, she wondered, could anticipate Mother Nature? What was to stop her from having a minor tantrum and perhaps heaving down a couple of boulders at the car? And since it was big enough to sleep eight, it was a dandy target.

M.J. kept a wary eye out of the side window, willing the rocks to stay put until they were through the pass.

Ahead, mountains rose and rolled, lushly green

with summer. Heat and humidity merged to make the air thick as syrup. Tires hummed along the highway.

Occasionally she would see houses behind the roadside trees, glimpses only, as if they were hiding from prying eyes. She wondered about them, those tucked-away houses, undoubtedly with neat yards guarded by yapping dogs, decorated with gardens and swing sets, accented with decks and patios for grills and redwood chairs.

It was one way to live, she supposed. But you had to tend that garden, mow that lawn.

She'd never lived in a house. Apartments had always suited her lifestyle. To some, she supposed, an apartment would seem like a box tucked with other boxes within a box. But she'd always been satisfied with her own space, with the camaraderie of being part of the hive.

Why would you need a lawn and a swing set unless you had kids?

She felt a quick little jitter in her stomach at the idea. Had she actually ever thought about having children before? Rocking a baby, watching it grow, tying shoes and wiping noses.

It was Grace who was soft on children, she thought. Not that she herself didn't like them. She had a platoon of cousins who seemed bent on populating the world, and M.J. had spent many an hour on a visit home cooing over a new baby, playing on the floor with a toddler or pitching a ball to a fledgling Little Leaguer.

She didn't imagine it was quite the same when the

child was yours. What did it feel like, she mused, to have your own baby rest its head on your shoulder and yawn, or to have a shaky-legged toddler lift its arms up to you to be held?

And what in God's name was she doing thinking about children at a time like this? Weary, she slipped her fingers under her shaded glasses, pressed them to her eyes.

Then slid a considering glance at Jack's profile. What, she wondered, did he think about kids?

Incredibly, she felt heat rising to her cheeks, and turned her face back to the window quickly. Idiot, she told herself. You've known the guy an instant, and you're starting to think of diapers and booties.

That, she thought grimly, was just what happened to a woman when she got herself tied up over some man. She went soft all over, particularly in the head.

Then she let out a shout that surprised them both. "There! That's the exit! That's where we got off. I'm sure of it."

"Next time just shoot me," Jack suggested as he swung the car into the right lane. "It's bound to be less of a shock than a heart attack."

"Sorry."

He eased off the exit, giving her time to orient herself as they came to a two-lane road.

"Left," she said after a moment. "I'm almost sure we went left."

"Okay, I need to gas up this hog, anyway." He headed for the closest service station and pulled up next to the pumps. "What was on your mind back there, M.J.?"

"On my mind?"

"You went away for a while."

The fact that he'd been able to tell disconcerted her. She shifted in the seat, shrugged her shoulders. "I was just concentrating, that's all."

"No, you weren't." He cupped a hand under her chin, turned her face to his. "That's exactly what you weren't doing." He rubbed his thumb over her lips. "Don't worry. We'll find your friends. They're going to be all right."

She nodded, felt a wash of shame. Grace and Bailey should have been on her mind, and instead she'd been daydreaming over babies like some lovesick idiot. "Grace will be at the house. All we have to do is find it."

"Hold that thought." He leaned forward, touched his lips to hers. "And go buy me a candy bar."

"You've got all the dough."

"Oh, yeah." He got out, reached into his front pocket and pulled out a handful of bills. "Splurge," he suggested, "and buy yourself one, too."

"Gee, thanks, Daddy."

He grinned as she walked away, long legs striding, narrow hips twitching under snug denim. Hell of a package, he mused as he slipped the nozzle into the gas tank. He wasn't going to question the twist of fate that had dropped her into his life, and into his heart.

But he wondered how long it would be before she

did. People didn't stay in his life for long—they came and went. It had been that way for so long, he'd stopped expecting it to be different. Maybe he'd stopped wanting it to be.

Still, he knew that if she decided to take a walk, he'd never get over it. So he'd have to make sure she didn't take a walk.

Feeding the greedy tank of the Olds, he watched her come back out, cross to the soft-drink machine. And he wasn't the only one watching, Jack noted. The teenager fueling the rusting pickup at the next pump had an eye on her, too.

Can't blame you, buddy, Jack thought. She's a picture, all right. Maybe you'll grow up lucky and find yourself a woman half as perfect for you.

And blessing his luck, Jack screwed the cap back on his tank, then strolled over to her. She had her hands full of candy and soft drinks when he yanked her against him and covered her mouth in a long, smoldering, brain-draining kiss.

Her breath whooshed out when he released her. "What was that for?"

"Because I can," he said simply, and all but swaggered in to pay his tab.

M.J. shook her head, noted that the teenager was gawking and had overfilled his tank. "I wouldn't light a match, pal," she said as she passed him and climbed into the car.

When Jack joined her, she went with impulse, plunging her hands into his hair and pulling him against her to kiss him in kind.

"That's because I can, too."

"Yeah." He was pretty sure he felt smoke coming out of his ears. "We're a hell of a pair." It took him a moment to clear the lust from his mind and remember how to turn the key.

Both thrilled and amused by his reaction, she held out a chocolate bar. "Candy?"

He grunted, took it, bit in. "Watch the road," he told her. "Try to find something familiar."

"I know we weren't on this road very long," she began. "We turned off and did a lot of snaking around on back roads. Like I said, Bailey had it all in her head. Bailey!" As the idea slammed into her, she pressed her hands to her mouth.

"What is it?"

"I kept asking myself where she would go. If she was in trouble, if she was running, where would she go?" Eyes alight, she whirled to face him. "And the answer is right there. She knows how to get to Grace's place. She loved it there. She'd feel safe there."

"It's a possibility," he agreed.

"No, no, she'd go to one of us for sure." She shook her head fiercely, desperately. "And she couldn't get to me. That means she headed up here, maybe took a bus or a train as far as she could, rented a car." Her heart lightened at the certainty of it. "Yes, it's logical, and just like her. They're both there, up in the woods, sitting there figuring out what to do next and worrying about me."

And so was he worrying about her. She was putting all her hope into a long shot, but he didn't have the heart to say it. "If they are," he said cautiously, "we still have to find them. Think back, try to remember."

"Okay." With new enthusiasm, she scanned the scenery. "It was spring," she mused. "It was pretty. Stuff was blooming—dogwoods, I guess, and that yellow bush that's almost a neon color. And something Bailey called redbuds. There was a garden place," she remembered suddenly. "A whatchama-callit, nursery. Bailey wanted to stop and buy Grace a bush or something. And I said we should get there first and see what she already had."

"So we look for a nursery."

"It had a dopey name." She closed her eyes a moment, struggled to bring it back. "Corny. It was right on the road, and it was packed. That's one of the reasons I didn't want to stop. It would have taken forever. Buds 'N' Blooms." She smacked her hands together as she remembered. "We made a right a mile or so beyond it."

"There you go." He took her hand, lifted it to his mouth to kiss. And had them both frowning at the gesture. He'd never kissed a woman's hand before in his entire life.

Inside M.J.'s stomach, butterflies sprang to life. Clearing her throat, she laid her hand on her lap. "Well, ah... Anyway, Grace and Bailey went back to the plant place. I stayed at her house. Those two get a big bang out of shopping. For anything. I figured they'd buy out the store—which they almost did. They came back loaded with those plastic trays of flowers, and flowers in pots, and a couple of bushes. Grace keeps a pickup at her place. I can imagine what they'd write in the *Post*'s style section about Grace Fontaine driving a pickup truck."

"Would she care?"

"She'd laugh. But she keeps this place to herself. The relatives—that's what she calls her family, the relatives—don't even know about it."

"I'd say that's to our favor. The less people who know about it, the better." His lips curved as he noted a sign. "There's your garden spot, sugar. Business is pretty good, even this late in the year."

Delight zinged through her as she spotted the line of cars and trucks pulled to the side of the road, the crowds of people wandering around tables covered with flowers. "I bet they're having a holiday sale. Ten percent off any red, white or blue posies."

"God bless America. About a mile, you said?"

"Yeah, and it was a right. I'm sure of that."

"Don't you like flowers?"

"Huh?" Distracted, she glanced at him. "Sure, they're okay. I like ones that smell. You know, like those things, those carnations. They don't smell like sissies, and they don't wimp out on you after a couple days, either."

He chuckled. "Muscle flowers. Is this the turn?"

"No…I don't think so. A little farther." Leaning forward, she tapped her fingers on the dash. "This is it, coming up. I'm almost sure."

He downshifted, bore right. The road rose and

curved. Beside it fences were being slowly smothered by honeysuckle, and behind them cows grazed.

"I think this is right." She gnawed on her lip. "All the damn roads back here look the same. Fields and rocks and trees. How do people find where they're going?"

"Did you stay on this road?"

"No, she turned again." Right or left? M.J. asked herself. Right or left? "We kept heading deeper into the boonies, and climbing. Maybe here."

He slowed, let her consider. The crossroads was narrow, cornered on one side by a stone house. A dog napped in the yard under the shade of a dying maple. Concrete ducks paddled over the grass.

"This could be it, to the left. I'm sorry, Jack, it's hazy."

"Look, we've got a full tank of gas and plenty of daylight. Don't sweat it."

He took the left, cruised along the curving road that climbed and dipped. The houses were spread out now, and the fields were crammed with corn high as a man's waist. Where fields stopped, woods took over, growing thick and green, arching their limbs over the road so that it was a shady tunnel for the car to thread through.

They came to the rise of a hill, and the world opened up. A dramatic and sudden spread of green mountains, and land that rolled beneath them.

"Yes. Bailey almost wrecked the car when we topped this hill. If it is this hill," she added. "I think that's part of the state forest. She was dazzled by it.

But we turned off again. One of these little roads that winds through the trees.''

"You're doing fine. Tell me which one you want to try."

"At this point, your guess is as good as mine." She felt helpless, stupid. "It just looks different now. The trees are all thick. They just had that green haze on them when we came through."

"We'll give this one a shot," he decided, and, flipping a mental coin, turned right.

It took only ten minutes for them to admit they were lost, and another ten to find their way out and onto a main road. They drove through a small town M.J. had no recollection of, then backtracked.

After an hour of wandering, M.J. felt her patience fraying. "How can you stay so calm?" she asked him. "I swear we've fumbled along every excuse for a road within fifty miles. Every street, lane and cow path. I'm going crazy."

"My line of work takes patience. I ever tell you about tracking down Big Bill Bristol?"

She shifted in her seat, certain she'd never feel sensation in her bottom again. "No, you never told me about tracking down Big Bill Bristol. Are you going to make this up?"

"Don't have to." To give them both a breather, he swung off the road. There was a small pulloff beside what he supposed could be called a swimming hole. Trees overhung dark water and let little splashes of sun hit the surface and bounce back. "Big Bill was up on assault. Lost his temper over a hand of seven-card stud and tried to feed the pot to his opponent. That was after he broke his nose and knocked the guy out. Big Bill is about six-five, two-eighty, and has hands the size of Minneapolis. He doesn't like to lose. I know this for a fact, as I have spent the occasional evening playing games of chance with Big Bill."

M.J. smiled winningly. "Gosh, Jack, I just can't wait to meet your friends."

Recognizing sarcasm when it was aimed at him, he merely slanted her a look. "In any case, Ralph fronted his bond, but Big Bill found out about a floating game in Jersey and didn't want to miss out. The law frowns, not only on floating games, but on bail-jumping, and his bail was revoked. Bill was on the skip list."

"And you went after him."

"Well, I did." Jack rubbed his chin, thought fleetingly about shaving. "It should have been cut-and-dried. Find the game, remind Bill he had to have his day in court, bring him back. But it seemed Bill had won large quantities of money in Jersey, and had moved on to another game. I should add that Bill is big, but not in the brain department. And he was on a hot streak, moving from game to game, state to state."

"With Jack Dakota, bounty hunter, hot on his trail."

"On his trail, anyway. A lot of it his back trail. If the jerk had planned to lose me, he couldn't have done a better job. I crisscrossed the Northeast, hit every game.''

"How much did you lose?"

"Not enough to talk about." He answered her grin. "I got into Pittsburgh about midnight. I knew there was a game, but I couldn't bribe or threaten the location out of anyone. I'd been on Bill's trail for four days, living out of my car and playing poker with guys named Bats and Fast Charlie. I was tired, dirty, down to my last hundred in cash. I walked into a bar."

"Of course you did."

"I'm telling the story," he said, tugging her hair. "Picked it at random, no thought, no plan. And guess who was in the back room, holding a pair of bullets and bumping the pot?"

"Let's see.... Could it have been...Big Bill Bristol?"

"In the flesh. Patience and logic had gotten me to Pittsburgh, but it was instinct that had me walking into that game."

"How'd you get him to go back with you?"

"There I had a choice. I considered hitting him over the head with a chair. But more than likely that would have just annoyed him. I thought about appealing to his good nature, reminding him he owed Ralph. But he was still on that hot streak, and wouldn't have given a damn. So I had a drink, joined the game. After a couple of hours, I explained the situation to Bill, and appealed to him on his own level. One cut of the cards. I draw high, he comes back with me, no hassle. He draws high, I walk away.''

''And you drew high?''

''Yeah, I did.'' He scratched his chin again. ''Of course, I'd palmed an ace, but like I said, brains weren't Big Bill's strong suit.''

''You cheated?''

''Sure. It was the clearest route through the situation, and everybody ended up happy.''

''Except Big Bill.''

''No, him, too. He'd had a nice run, had enough of the ready to pay off the guy whose skull he'd cracked. Charges dropped. No sweat.''

She cocked her head. ''And what would you have done if he'd decided to welsh and not go back with you peacefully?''

''I'd have broken the chair over his head, and hoped to live through it.''

''Quite a life you lead, Jack.''

''I like it. And the moral of the story is, you just keep looking, follow logic. And when logic peters out, you go with instinct.'' So saying, he reached into his pocket, drew out the stone. ''The second stone is knowledge.'' His eyes met hers. ''What do you know, M.J.?''

''I don't understand.''

''You know your friends. You know them better than I know Big Bill, or anyone else, for that matter.'' He could come to envy her that, he realized. And would think on it more closely later. ''They're part of what you were, who you are, and, I guess, who you will be.''

Her chest went tight. ''You're getting philosophical on me, Dakota.''

''Sometimes that works, too. Trust your instincts, M.J.'' He took her hand, closed it over the stone. ''Trust what you know.''

Her nerves were suddenly on the surface of her skin, chilling it. ''You expect me to use this thing like some sort of compass? Divining rod?''

''You feel that, don't you?'' It was a shock to him, as well, but his hands stayed steady, his eyes remained on hers. ''It's all but breathing. You know the thing about myths? If you reach down deep enough inside them, you pull out truth. The second stone is knowledge.'' He shifted back, put his hands on the wheel. ''Which way do you want to go?''

She was cold, shudderingly cold. Yet the stone was like a sun burning in her hand. ''West.'' She heard herself say it, knew it was odd for a city woman to use the direction, rather than simply right or left. ''This is crazy.''

''We left sanity behind yesterday. No use trying to find that back trail. Just tell me which way you want to go. Which way feels right.''

So she held the stone gripped in her hand and directed him through the winding roads sided with trees and outcroppings of rock. Along a meandering stream that trickled low from lack of rain, past a little brown house so close that its door all but opened into the road.

"On the right," M.J. said, through a throat dust-dry and tight as a drum. "You have to watch for it. We passed it, had to double back. Her lane's narrow, just a cut through the woods. You can barely see it. She doesn't have a mailbox. She goes into town and picks it up when she's here. There." her hand trembled a bit as she pointed. "Just there."

He turned in. The lane was indeed narrow. Branches skimmed and scraped along the sides of the car as he drove slowly up, over gravel, around a curve that was sheltered by more trees.

And there, in the center of the lane, still as a stone statue, stood a deer with a pelt that glowed dark gold in the flash of sun.

It should be a white hind, Jack thought foolishly. A white hind is the symbol of a quest.

The doe watched the lumbering approach, her head up, her eyes wide and fixed. Then, with a flick of the tail, a quick spin of that gorgeous body, she leaped into the trees on thin, graceful legs. And was gone with barely a rustle.

The house was exactly as M.J. remembered. Tucked back on the hill, above a small, bubbling creek, it was a neat two stories that blended into the backdrop of woods. It was wood and glass, simple lines, with a long front porch painted a bold blue. Two white rockers sat on it, along with copper pots overflowing with trailing flowers.

"She's been busy," M.J. murmured, scanning the gardens. Flowers bloomed everywhere, wildly, as if unplanned. The flow of colors and shapes tumbled down the hill like a river. Wide wooden steps cut through the color, meandered to the left, then marched down to the lane.

"At the house in Potomac she hired a professional landscaper. She knew just what she wanted, but she had someone else do it. Here, she wanted to do everything herself."

"It looks like a fairy tale." He shifted, uncomfortable with his own impressions. He wasn't exactly up on his fairy tales. "You know what I mean."

"Yeah."

A shiny blue pickup truck was parked at the end of the lane. But there was no sign of the car Grace would have driven to her country home. No dusty rental car announcing Bailey's presence.

They've just gone to the store, M.J. told herself. They'll be back any minute.

She wouldn't believe they'd come this far, found the house, and not found Grace and Bailey.

The minute Jack pulled up beside the truck, she was out and dashing toward the house.

"Hold it." He gripped her arm, skidded her to a halt. "Let's get the lay of the land here." Gently he uncurled her fingers, took the stone. When it was tucked back in his pocket, he took her hand. "You said she leaves the truck here?"

"Yes. She drives a Mercedes convertible, or a little Beemer."

"Your pal has three rides?"

"Grace rarely owns one of anything. She claims

she doesn't know what she's going to be in the mood for.''

''There's a back door?''

''Yeah, one out the kitchen, and another on the side.'' She gestured to the right, fought to ignore the weight pressing against her chest. ''It leads onto a little patio and into the woods.''

''Let's look around first.''

There was a gardening shed, neatly filled with tools, a lawn mower, rakes and shovels. Where the lawn gave way, stepping-stones had been set, with springy moss growing between. More flowers—a raised bed with blooms and greenery spilling over the dark wall, and the cliff behind growing with ivy.

A hummingbird hovered at a bright red feeder, its iridescent wings blurred with speed. It darted off like a bullet at their approach, its whirl the only sound.

He spotted no broken windows or other signs of forced entry as they circled around the back, passed an herb garden fragrant with scents of rosemary and mint. Brass wind chimes hung silently near the rear door. Not a leaf stirred.

''It's creepy.'' She rubbed her arm. ''Skulking around like this.''

''Let's just skulk another minute.''

They came around the far side with the little patio. There, a glass table, a padded chaise, more flowers in concrete troughs and clay pots. Just beyond was a small pond with young ornamental grasses.

''That's new.'' M.J. paused to study. ''She didn't

have that before. She talked about it, though. It looks fresh.''

"I'd say your pal's done some planting this week. You think there's a plant or flower in existence she's missed?''

"Probably not." But M.J.'s smile was weak as they came back around to the front. "I want to go in, Jack. I have to go in.''

"Let's take a look." He climbed the porch steps, found the front door locked. "She got a hidey-hole for a key?''

"No." Despite the miserable heat, she rubbed her hands over her chilled arms. Too quiet, was all she could think. It was much too quiet. "She used to keep an extra for the Potomac house, in this flower-pot outside the door, but her cousin Melissa found it and made herself at home while Grace was in Milan. Really ticked her off.''

He crouched, examined the locks. "She's got good ones. Simpler to break a window.''

"You're not breaking one of her windows.''

He sighed, rose. "I was afraid you'd say that. Okay, we do it the hard way.''

While she frowned, he went back to his car, popped the trunk. Inside, it was loaded with tools, clothes, books, water jugs and paperwork. He pushed around, selected what he needed.

"Does she have an alarm system?''

"No. Not that I know of, anyway." M.J. studied the leather pouch. "What are you going to do?''

"Pop the locks. It may take a while, I'm rusty.''

But he rubbed his hands together, anticipating the challenge. "You could go around, check the other doors and windows, just in case she left something unlocked."

"If she locked one, she locked them all. But okay."

She circled around again, pausing at each window, tugging, then peering in. By the time she'd made a complete circuit, Jack was on the second lock.

Intrigued, she watched him finesse it. It was cooler here than in the city, but the heat was still nasty. Sweat dampened his shirt, gleamed on his throat.

"Can you teach me to do that?" she asked him.

"Ssh!" He wiped his hands on his jeans, took a firmer hold on his pick. "Got it." He stood, swiped an arm over his brow. "Cold shower," he murmured. "Cold beer. I'll kiss your pal's feet if she's got both."

"Grace doesn't drink beer." But M.J. was pushing in the door ahead of him.

The living area was homey, tidy but still lived-in, with its wide striped sofa, the deep chairs that picked up the rich blue tones. In the brick fireplace, a lush green fern rose out of a brass spittoon.

M.J. moved quickly through the rooms, over wide-planked chestnut floors and Berber rugs, into the sunny kitchen, with its forest green counters and white tiles, through to the cozy parlor Grace had turned into a library.

The house seemed to echo around her, as she raced upstairs, looked in the bedrooms, the baths.

Grace's gleaming brass bed was tidily made, the handmade lace spread she'd purchased in Ireland accented with rich dots of colorful pillows. A book on gardening lay on the nightstand.

The bathroom was empty, the ivory shell of the sink scrubbed clean and shining in its powder blue counter. Towels were neatly folded on the shelves on a tall wicker stand.

Knowing it was useless, she looked in the bedroom closet. It was ridiculously full and ruthlessly organized.

"They're not here, M.J." Jack touched her shoulder, but she jerked away.

"I can see that, can't I?" Her voice snapped out, broke like a rigid twig. "But Grace was here. She was just here. I can still smell her." She closed her eyes, drew in the air. "Her perfume. It hasn't faded yet. That's her scent. Some fragrance tycoon who fell for her had it designed for her. I can smell her in here."

"Okay." He caught the scent himself, classy sex with wild undertones. "Maybe she ran into town for supplies, or took a drive."

"No." She walked away from him, toward the window as she spoke. "She wouldn't have locked the house up for that. She always says how lovely it is not to worry about locking up out here. She only does when she closes the place up and heads somewhere else. Bailey isn't here. Grace isn't here, and she's not planning on coming back for a while. We've missed her."

"Back to Potomac?"

She shook her head. The tightness in her chest was unbearable, as if greedy hands were squeezing her heart and lungs. "Not likely. She'd avoid the city on the Fourth. Too much traffic, too many tourists. That's why I was sure she'd stay through until tomorrow at least. She could be anywhere."

"Which means she'll surface somewhere." He started toward her, caught the gleam on her cheek and stopped dead, like a man who'd run facefirst into a glass wall. "What are you doing? Are you crying?" It was an accusation, delivered in a voice edged with abject terror.

M.J. merely wrapped her arms over her chest and hugged her elbows. All the excitement, the tension, the frustration, of the search fell away into sheer despair.

The house was empty.

"I want you to stop that. Right now. I mean it. Sniveling isn't going to do you any good." And it certainly wasn't going to do him any good. It terrified him, left him feeling stupid, clumsy and annoyed.

"Just leave me alone," she said, and her voice broke on a muffled sob. "Just go away."

"That's just what I'm going to do. You keep that up, and I'm walking. I mean it. I'm not standing around and watching you blubber. Get a grip on yourself. Haven't you got any pride?"

At the moment, pride was low on her list. Giving up, she pressed her brow to the window glass and let the tears fall.

"I'm walking, M.J." He snarled at her and turned for the door. "I'm getting a drink and a shower. So when you've got yourself in order, we'll figure out what to do next."

"Then go. Just go."

He made it as far as the threshold, then, swearing ripely, whirled back. "I don't need this," he muttered.

He hadn't a clue how to handle a woman's tears, particularly those from a strong woman who was obviously at the end of her endurance. He cursed her again as he turned her into his arms, folded her into them. He continued to swear at her as he picked her up, sat with her in a wide-backed chair.

He rocked and cursed and stroked.

"Get it over with, then." Kissed her temple. "Please. You're killing me."

"I'm afraid." Her breath hitched as she turned her face into his shoulder. His strong, broad shoulder. "I'm so tired and afraid."

"I know." He kissed her hair, held her closer. "I know."

"I couldn't stand for anything to happen to them. I just can't bear it."

"Don't." He tightened his grip, as if he could strangle off those hot, terrifying tears. But his mouth skimmed up her cheek, found hers, and was tender. "It's going to be all right. Everything's going to be all right." He brushed at her tears clumsily with his thumbs. "I promise."

Eyes brimming, she stared into his. "I was just so sure they'd be here."

"I know." He brushed the hair back from her face. "You've got a right to break down. I don't know anyone else who'd have made it this far without a blowout. But don't cry anymore, M.J. It rips me up."

"I hate to cry." She sniffled, knuckled tears away.

"I'm glad to hear it." He took her hands, kissed them both this time, without that moment of surprise. "Think about this. She was here today, maybe as little as an hour ago. She's tidied up, locked up. Which means she was just fine when she left."

She let out an unsteady breath, drew in another. "You're right. I'm not thinking straight."

"That's because you need a break. A decent meal, a little rest."

"Yeah." But she laid her head against his shoulder again. "Can we just sit here for a little while. Just sit like this?"

"Sure." It was easy to wrap his arms around her, hold her close. And just sit.

Chapter 10

He told her it didn't make sense to drive back to the city, fight the traffic generated by fireworks fans. Not when they had a perfectly good place to stay the night.

The fact was, he thought, if she'd broken down once, she could easily do so again. And a decent meal, along with a decent night's sleep, might shore up some holes in her composure.

In any case, they'd been in the car for more than five hours that day already, after little more than an hour's sleep. Driving straight back was bound to make them both feel as though the effort to find Grace's house had been wasted.

And he wanted time to work on a plan that was beginning to form in his mind.

''Take a shower,'' he told her. ''Borrow a shirt or something from your pal. You'll feel better.''

''It couldn't hurt.'' She managed a smile. ''I thought you wanted a shower? Don't you want to conserve water?''

''Well...'' It was tempting. He could envision himself getting under a cool spray with her, lathering up—lathering her up—and letting nature take its very interesting course.

And it also occurred to him that she hadn't had five full minutes of privacy in hours. It was about all he had the power to give her at the moment.

''I'm going to hunt up a drink. See if your friend has some cans around here I can open.'' He kissed the tip of her nose affectionately. ''Go ahead and get started without me.''

''Okay, you can hunt me up a drink while you're at it, but you're not going to find any beer in the fridge. And God knows what she's got in cans around here.''

M.J. headed for the bath, stopped, turned. ''Jack? Thanks for letting me get it out.''

He tucked his hands in his pockets. Her eyes, those exotically tilted cat's eyes, were still swollen from weeping, and her cheeks were pale with fatigue. ''I guess you needed to.''

''I did, and you didn't make me feel like too much of a jerk. So thanks,'' she said again, and stepped into the bath.

She stripped gratefully, all put peeling cotton and denim away from her clammy, overheated skin. The simple style Grace had chosen for the rest of the house didn't follow through to the master bath. This was pure self-indulgence.

The tiles were soft blue and misty green, so that it was like stepping into a cool seaside glade. The tub was an oversize lake of white, fueled with water jets and framed by a wide lip where more ferns grew lushly in biscuit-toned pots.

The acre of counter boasted a cutout for a vanity stool and held a brass makeup mirror. Overhead was a garden of tulip-shaped lights of frosted glass. Doors holding linens and sheet-size towels were mirrored, tossing the room back and giving the illusion of enormous, luxurious space.

Though M.J. briefly considered the tub, and the bubbling jets, she stepped instead toward the wavy glass block of the shower enclosure. Her shower-heads were set in three sides at varying levels. With a need for pampering, M.J. turned them all on full, then, after one enormous sigh, helped herself to some of Grace's pricey soap and shampoo.

And the fragrance made her weepy again. It was so Grace.

But she refused to cry, already regretted her earlier tears. They helped nothing. Practicalities did, she reminded herself. A shower, a meal, a respite from activity for a brief time, would all serve to clear the brain. Undoubtedly, she needed a few hours' sleep to recharge. It wasn't just the crying jag that made her feel woozy and weak, she imagined.

Something had to be done, some move had to be

made, and quickly. To make it, she needed to be sharp and to be ready.

It hardly mattered that it hadn't been much more than a day that had passed. Every hour she lived through without being able to contact either Bailey or Grace was one short, tense lifetime.

Things had to be settled, her world had to be set right again. And then she would have to face whatever was happening, and whatever would happen, between her and Jack.

She was in love with him, there was no doubt of that. The speed with which she'd fallen only increased the intensity of the emotion. She'd never felt for any man what she felt for him—this emotion that cut clean through the bone. And melded with the feeling of passion, which she could have dismissed, was a sense of absolute trust, an odd and deep affection, a prideful respect, and the certainty that she could pass the years of her life with him—if not in harmony, in contentment.

She understood him, she realized as she held her face under the highest spray. She doubted he knew that, but it was absolutely true. She understood his loneliness, his scarred-over pain, and his pride in his own skills.

He had kindness and cynicism, patience and impulse. He had a questing intellect, a touch of the poet—and more than a touch of the nonconformist. He lived his own way, making his own rules and breaking them when he chose.

She would have wanted no less in a life partner.

And that was what worried her. Finding herself thinking of marriage, permanence and making a family with a man who so obviously ran from all three, and had run from them most of his life.

But perhaps, since those concepts had bloomed so recently in her, she could nip them in the bud. She had a business of her own, a life of her own. Wanting Jack to be a part of that didn't have to change the basic order of things.

She hoped.

She switched off the showerheads, toweled off and, because it was there, slathered on some of Grace's silky body cream. And felt nearly human again. Rubbing a towel over her hair, she padded naked into the bedroom to raid the closet.

At least in the country Grace's choice of attire ran toward the simple. M.J. slipped on a short-sleeved shirt of minute white-and-blue checks and found a pair of cotton shorts in the bureau. They bagged a little. Grace was still built like the centerfold she'd once been, and M.J. had no hips to speak of. They also ran short, as M.J. had several inches more leg than her friend.

But they were cool, and when she slid them on she stopped feeling like a woman who'd been living in her clothes for two days.

She started to toss the towel aside, then rolled her eyes when she thought of how Grace would react to that. Fastidiously she went back to the bath and draped it over the shower. Then, in bare feet, her hair still damp and curling around her face, she went in search of Jack.

"I not only started without you," she said when she found him in the kitchen, "I finished without you. You're slow, Dakota."

Still frowning at the small jar in his hand, he turned. "All I found was..." And trailed off, staggered.

He'd told himself she wasn't beautiful, and that was true. But she was striking. The impact of her slammed into him anew, those sharp, sexy looks, the long, long legs set off by tiny blue shorts. She had her thumbs tucked in the front pockets of them, a half-cocked grin on her face, and her hair was dark and damp and curling foolishly over her ears.

His mouth simply watered.

"You clean up good, sugar."

"It's hard not to, in that fancy shower of Grace's. Wait till you get a load of it." She angled her head as a nice flush of heat began to work up from her toes. "I don't know why you're looking at me like that, Jack. You've seen me naked."

"Yeah. Maybe I've got a weakness for long women in little shorts." He lifted a brow. "Did you borrow any of her underwear?"

"No. Some things even close friends don't share. Men and underwear being the top two."

He set the jar down. "In that case—"

She shot a hand up, slapped in on his chest. "I don't think so, pal. You don't exactly smell like roses at the moment. And besides, I'm hungry."

"The woman gets cleaned up, she gets picky."
But he ran a hand over his chin again, reminded himself to get his shaving kit out of the trunk this time.
"There's not a hell of a lot to choose from around here. She's got fancy French bubbly in the fridge, more fancy French wine in a rack in the closet over there. Some crackers in tins, some pasta in glass jars. I found some tomato paste, which I guess is embryonic spaghetti sauce."

"Does that mean one of us has to cook?"

"I'm afraid it does."

They considered each other for ten full seconds.

"Okay," he decided. "We flip for it."

"Fair enough. Heads, you cook," she said as he dug out a quarter. "Tails, I cook. Either way, I have a feeling we'll be looking for her antacid."

She hissed when the quarter turned up tails. "Isn't there anything else? Something we can just eat out of a can or jar?"

"You cook," he said, but held out a jar. "And there's fish eggs."

She blew out a breath as she studied the jar of beluga. "You don't like caviar?"

"Give me a trout, fry it up, and that's dandy. What the hell do I want to eat eggs that some fish has laid?" But he tossed her the jar. "Help yourself. I'll go clean up while you do something with that tomato paste."

"You probably won't like it," she said darkly, but dug out a pan as he wandered off.

Thirty minutes later, he wandered in again. His

hair was slicked back, his face clean-shaven. The smells coming from the simmering pan weren't half-bad, he decided. The kitchen door was open, and there was M.J., sitting out on the patio, cramming a caviar-loaded cracker in her mouth.

"Not too bad," she said over it when she saw him. "You just pretend it's something else, then wash it down with this." She sipped champagne, shrugged. "Grace goes for this stuff. Always did. It was the way she was raised."

"Environment can twist a person," he agreed, then opened his mouth and let M.J. ram a cracker in. He grimaced, snagged her glass and downed it. "A hot dog and a nice dark beer."

She sighed, perfectly in tune with him. "Yeah, well, beggars can't be choosers, pal. It's nice out here. Cooled off some. But you know the trouble? You just can't hear anything. No traffic, no voices, no movement. It kind of creeps me out."

"People that live in places like this don't really like being around other people." He was hungry enough to load up a cracker for himself. "You and me, M.J., we're social animals. We're at our best in a crowded room."

"Yeah, that's why I work the pub most nights. I like the busy hours." She brooded, looking off to where the sun was sinking fast behind the trees. "Tonight would be slow. Sunday, holiday. Everybody'll be wondering where I am. I've got a good head waitress, though. She'll handle it."

She shifted restlessly, reached for her glass. "I

guess the cops have gone by, talked to her and my bartenders, some of the regulars. They'll be worried.''

"It won't take much longer." He'd been working on refining his plan, looking for the pitfalls. "Your pub'll run a few days without you. You take vacations, right?"

"A couple weeks here and there."

"It's supposed to be Paris next."

She was surprised he remembered. "That's the plan. Have you ever been there?"

"No, have you?

"Nope. We went to Ireland when I was a kid, and my father got all misty-eyed and sentimental. He grew up on the West Side of Manhattan, but you'd have thought he'd been born and bred in Dublin and had been wrenched away by Gypsies. Other than that, I've never been out of the States."

"I've been up to Canada, down to Mexico, but I've never flown over the ocean." He smiled and took the glass from her again. "I think your sauce is burning, sugar."

She swore, shot up and scrambled inside. While she muttered, he eyed the level of the bottle. Normally he wouldn't have recommended alcohol as a tranquilizer, but these were desperate times. He'd seen that misery come into her eyes when he mentioned Paris—and reminded her of her friends.

For a few hours, for this one night, he was going to make her forget.

"I caught it in time," she told him, dragging her

hair back as she stepped out again. "And I put on the water for the pasta. I don't know how long that sauce is supposed to cook—probably for three days, but we're eating it rare."

He grinned, handed her the glass he'd just topped off. "Fine with me. There was another bottle of this chilling, right?"

"Yeah, I get it for her by the case. My distributor just loves it." She knocked some back, chuckled into the exquisite bubbles. "I can imagine what my customers would say if I put Brother Dom on the menu."

"I'm getting used to it." He rose, skimmed a hand over her hair. "I'm going to put some music on. Too damn quiet around here."

"Good idea." With a considering look, she glanced over her shoulder. "You know, I think Grace said they have, like, bears and things up here."

He looked dubiously into the woods. "Guess I'll get my gun, too."

He got more than that. To her surprise, he brought candles into the kitchen, turned the stereo on low and found a station that played blues. He stuck a pink flower that more or less resembled a carnation to him behind her ear.

"Yeah, I guess redheads can wear pink," he decided after a smiling study. "You look cute."

Blowing her hair out of her eyes, she drained the pasta. "What's this? A romantic streak?"

"I've got one I keep in reserve." And while her

hands were full, he leaned in and nuzzled the back of her neck. "Does that bother you?"

"No." She angled her head, enjoying the leaping thrill up her spine. "But to complete the mood, you're going to have to eat this and pretend it's good." She frowned a little when he retrieved another bottle of champagne from the refrigerator. "Do you know what that costs a bottle, ace? Even wholesale?"

"Beggars can't be choosers," he reminded her, and popped the cork.

As meals went, they'd both had better—and worse. The pasta was only slightly overdone, the sauce was bland but inoffensive. And, being ravenous, they dipped into second helpings without complaint.

He made certain he steered the conversation away from anything that worried her.

"Probably should have used some of those herbs she's got growing out there," M.J. considered. "But I don't know what's what."

"It's fine." He took her hand, pressed a kiss to the palm, and made her blink. "How are you feeling?"

"Better." She picked up her glass. "Full."

Nerves? Funny, he thought, she hadn't shown nerves when he handcuffed her, or when he drove like a madman through the streets of Washington with potential killers on their tail.

But nuzzle her hand and she looked edgy as a

virgin bride on her wedding night. He wondered just how much more nervous he could make her.

"I like looking at you," he murmured.

She sipped hastily, set the glass down, picked it up again. "You've been looking at me for two days."

"Not in candlelight." He filled her glass again. "It puts fire in your hair. In your eyes. Star fire." He smiled slowly, held the glass out to her. "What's that line? 'Fair as a star, when only one is shining in the sky.'"

"Yeah." She gulped wine, felt it fizz in her throat. "I think that's it."

"You're the only one, M.J." He pushed the plates aside so that he could nibble on her fingers. "Your hand's trembling."

"It is not." Her heart was, but she tugged her hand free, just in case he was right. She drank again, then narrowed her eyes. "Are you trying to get me drunk, Dakota?"

His smile was slow, confident. "Relaxed. And you were relaxed, M.J. Before I started to seduce you."

A hot ball of need lodged in the pit of her stomach. "Is that what you call it?"

"You're ripe for seducing." He turned her hand over, grazed his teeth over the inside of her wrist. "Your head's swimming with wine, your pulse is unsteady. If you were to stand right now, your legs would be weak."

She didn't have to stand for them to be weak. Even

sitting, her knees were shaking. "I don't need to be seduced. You know that."

"What I know is that I'm going to enjoy it. I want you trembling, and weak, and mine."

She was afraid she already was, and pulled back, unnerved. "This is silly. If you want to go to bed—"

"We'll get there. Eventually." He rose, drew her to her feet, then slid his hands in one long, possessive stroke down the sides of her body. Then back up. "You're worried about what I can do to you."

"You don't worry me."

"Yes, I do." He eased her against him, kept his mouth hovering over hers a moment, then lowered it to nip lightly at her jaw. "Just now I worry you a lot."

Her breath was thick, unsteady. "Cook a man one meal and he gets delusions of grandeur." And when he chuckled, his breath warm on her cheek, she shivered. "Kiss me, Jack." Her mouth turned, seeking his. "Just kiss me."

"You're not afraid of the fire." He evaded her lips, heard her moan as his mouth skimmed her throat. "But the warmth unnerves you. You can have both." His lips brushed hers, retreated. "Tonight, we'll have both. There won't be any choice."

The wine was swimming in her head, just as he'd said. In sparkling circles. She was trembling, just as he'd said. In quick, helpless quivers.

And she was weak, just as he'd said.

Even as she strained for the fire, the flash danced out of her reach. There was only the warmth, enervating, sweet, drugging. Her breath caught, then released in a rush when he lifted her.

"Why are you doing this?"

"Because you need it," he murmured. "And so do I."

He heated her skin with nibbling kisses as he carried her from the room. Filled his head with the scent that was foreign to both of them and only added to the mystery.

The house was dark, empty, with the silvery shower of moonlight guiding his path up the steps. He laid her on the bed, covered her with his body. And finally, finally, lowered his mouth to hers.

Her limbs went weak as the kiss drained her, sent her floating. She struggled once, tried to find level ground. But he deepened the kiss so slowly, so cleverly, so tenderly, she simply slid into the velvet trap he'd already laid for her.

She murmured his name, heard the echo of it whisper through her head. And surrendered.

He felt the change, that soft and complete yielding. The gift of it was powerfully arousing, sent dark ripples of delight dancing through his blood. Even as his desire quickened, his mouth slipped down to gently explore the pulse that beat so hard and thick in the hollow of her throat.

"Let go," he said quietly. "Just let go of everything, and let me take you."

His hands were gentle on her, skimming and tracing those curves and angles. This, he thought, makes her sigh. And that makes her moan. As if their time were endless, he tutored himself in the pleasures of her. The strong curve of her shoulder, the long muscles of her thigh, the surprisingly fragile line of her throat.

He undressed her slowly, pressing his lips to the hands that reached for him until they went limp again.

He left her nothing to hold on to but trust. Gave her nothing to experience but pleasure. Tenderness destroyed her, until her world was whittled down to the slowly rising storm inside her own body.

The fire was there, that flash of lightning and outrageous heat, the whip of wind and roll of power. But he held it off with clever hands and patient mouth, easing her along the path he'd chosen for them.

He turned her over, and those hands stroked the muscles in her shoulders and turned them to liquid. That mouth traced kisses down her spine and made her quake even as her mind went misty.

She could hear the rustle of the sheets as he moved over her, hear the whisper of his promises, feel the warm glow of promises kept.

And from outside, in the deepening night, came the long haunting call of an owl.

No part of her body was ignored. No aspect of seduction forgotten. She lay helpless beneath him, open to any demand. And when demand finally came, her moan was long, throaty, the response of her body instant and full.

He buried his face between her breasts, fighting

back the urge to rush, now that he'd brought her so luxuriously to the peak.

"I want more of you," he murmured. "I want all of you. I want everything."

He closed his mouth over her breast until she moved under him again, until her breath was nothing but feverish little pants. When her voice broke on his name, he slipped inside her, filled her slowly.

Teetering on a new brink, she arched toward him. Her eyes locked on his as they linked hands. There was only his face in the moonlight, dark eyes, firm mouth, the rich flow of hair threaded with gold.

Swept by a rushing tide of love, she smiled up at him. "Take more of me." She felt his fingers tremble in hers. "Take all of me." Saw the flash that was both triumph and need in his eyes. "Take everything."

The fire reached out for both of them.

While she slept, he held her close against him and worked out the final points of his plan. It had as much chance of working, he'd decided, as it did of blowing up in his face.

Even odds weren't such a bad deal.

He'd have risked much worse for her, much more to prevent those tears from slipping down her cheeks again. He'd waited thirty years to fall, which, he concluded, was why he'd fallen so hard, and so fast.

Unless he wanted to take the more mystical route and believe it was all simply fated—the timing, the stone, M.J. Either way, he'd come to the same place.

She was the first and only person he'd ever loved, and there was nothing he wouldn't do to protect her.

Even if it meant breaking her trust.

If this was the last time he'd lie beside her, he could hardly complain. She'd given him more in two days than he'd had in his entire life.

She loved him, and that answered all the questions.

As Jack lay in the deep country dark, contemplating his life, wondering about his future, another sat in a room washed with light. His day had been full, and now he was weary. But his mind wouldn't shut off, and he couldn't afford the fatigue.

He had watched fireworks streak across the sky. He had smiled, conversed, sipped fine wine. But all the while the rage had eaten at him, like a cancer.

Now, he was blessedly alone, in the room that soothed his soul. He feasted his eyes on the Renoir. Such lovely, subtle colors, he mused. Such exquisite brush strokes. And only he would ever look upon its magnificence.

There, the puzzle box of a Chinese emperor. Glossy with lacquer, a red dragon streaking over it and into a black sky. Priceless, full of secrets. And only he had the key.

Here, a ruby ring that had once graced the royal finger of Louis XIV. He slipped it on his pinkie, turned the stone toward the light and watched it shoot fire. From the king's hand to his, he thought. With a few detours along the way, but it was where it belonged now.

Usually such things brought him a deep, exquisite pleasure.

But not tonight.

Some had been punished, he thought. Some were beyond punishment. Yet it wasn't enough.

His treasure room was filled with the stunning, the unique, the ancient. Yet it wasn't enough.

The Three Stars were the only thing that would satisfy him. He would trade every treasure he owned for them. For with them, he would need nothing else.

The fools believed they understood them. Believed they could control them. And elude him. They were meant for him, of course. Their power was always meant for him.

And the loss of them was like ground glass in his throat.

He rose, ripping the ruby from his finger and flinging it across the room like a child tossing a broken toy. He would have them back. He was sure of it. But a sacrifice must be made. To the god, he thought with a slow smile. Of course, a sacrifice to the god.

In blood.

He left the room, leaving the lights burning. And most of his sanity behind.

Chapter 11

Jack considered leaving a note. When she woke, she'd be alone. At first, she'd probably assume he'd gone out to find that little store she'd spoken of, to buy some food.

She'd be impatient, a little annoyed. After an hour or so, she might worry that he'd gotten himself lost on the back roads.

But it wouldn't take her long to realize he was gone.

As he walked quietly down the stairs, just as dawn broke, he imagined her first reaction would be anger. She'd storm through the house, cursing him, threatening him. She'd probably kick something.

He was almost sorry to miss it.

She might even hate him for a while, he thought. But she'd be safe here. That was what mattered most.

He stepped outside, into the quiet mist of morning that shrouded the trees and hazed the sky. A few birds were up with him, stretching their vocal cords. Grace's flowers perfumed the air like a fantasy, and there was dew on the grass. He saw a deer, likely the same doe that had been on the lane the day before, standing at the edge of the woods.

They studied each other a moment, each both interested in and wary of the alien species. Then, dismissing him, she moved with hardly a sound along the verge of the trees, until she was slowly swallowed by them.

He glanced back at the house where he'd left M.J. sleeping. If everything went as he hoped, he'd be back for her by nightfall. It would take some doing, he knew, but he had to believe he'd convince her—eventually—that he'd acted for the best. And if her feelings were hurt, well, hurt feelings weren't terminal.

Again, he considered leaving a note—something short and to the point. But he decided against it. She'd figure it out for herself quickly enough. She was a sharp woman.

His woman, he thought as he slipped behind the wheel of the car. Whatever happened to him in the course of this day, she would be safe.

A soldier prepared for battle, a knight armed for the charge, he steeled himself to leave his lady and ride off into the mist. Such was his mood when he turned the key and the engine responded with a dull click.

His mood deflated like a sail emptied of wind.

Terrific, great, just what he needed. He swung out of the car, resisted slamming the door, and rounded the hood. Muttering oaths, he popped it, stuck his head under.

"Lose something, ace?"

Slowly he withdrew his head from under the hood. She was standing on the porch, legs spread, hands fisted on her hips, venom in her eyes. It had taken only a glance to see that his distributor cap was missing. He didn't even need to look at her to conclude that she'd nailed him.

But he was cool. He'd faced down worse than one angry woman in his checkered career. "Looks that way. You're up early, M.J."

"So are you, Jack."

"I was hungry." He flashed a smile—and kept his distance. "I thought I'd hunt up some breakfast."

She cocked a brow. "Got your club in the car?"

"My club?"

"That's what Neanderthals do, don't they? Get their club and go off into the woods to bash a bear for meat."

As she came down the steps toward him, he kept the smile plastered to his face, leaned back on the fender. "I had something a little more civilized in mind. Something like bacon and eggs."

"Oh? And where are you going to find bacon and eggs around here at dawn?"

She had him there. "Ah...I thought I could, you

know, find a farmer and—'' The breath whooshed out of his lungs as her fist plunged into his belly.

''Don't you lie to me. Do I look stupid?''

He coughed, got his breath back and managed to straighten. ''No. Listen—''

''Did you think I couldn't tell what was going on last night? The way you made love to me? Did you think you'd soften me up so I wouldn't know that was a big goodbye scene? You bastard!'' She swung again, but this time he ducked, so she missed his jaw by inches.

Now his own temper began to climb. He'd never treated a woman with such care as he'd treated her with in the night, and now she was tossing it back in his face. ''What did you do, sneak down here in the middle of the night and sabotage my ride?''

He saw the answer to that in the thin, satisfied smile that spread on her face. ''Oh, that's nice. Real nice. Trusting.''

''How dare you talk about trust! You were going to leave me here.''

''Yeah, that's right. Now where's the distributor cap?'' He took her by the arms, firmly, before she could take another shot at him. ''Where is it?''

''Where do you think you're going? What sort of idiotic plan have you mapped out in that tiny, feeble brain of yours?''

''I'm going to take care of business,'' he said grimly. ''I'll come back for you when I'm done.''

''Come back for me? What am I, a pet?'' She jerked, but didn't manage to free herself until she'd hammered her heel onto his instep. "You're going back to the city, aren't you? You're going looking for trouble."

His fury was such that he wondered only briefly how many bones in his foot she might have broken. "I know what I'm doing. It's what I do. And what you're going to do is give me the cap, then you're going to wait."

"The hell I am. We started this together, and we finish it together."

"No." He swung her around until her back was pressed into the car. "I'm not taking any chances with you."

"Since when are you in charge? I take my own chances. Get your hands off me."

"No." He leaned in, cuffing her hands with his. "For once in your life, you're going to do what you're told. You're going to stay here. I can move faster without you, and I'll be damned if I'm going to be distracted worrying about you."

"Nobody's asking you to worry about me. Just what are you planning to do?"

"I've wasted enough time letting them chase me. It's time to flush them out, on my turf, my terms."

"You're going after those two maniacs in the van?" Her heart lodged in her throat and was ruthlessly swallowed. "Fine. Good idea. I'm going with you."

"You're staying here. They haven't found this place, and it doesn't look like they're going to. You'll be safe." He lifted her to her toes, shook her.

"M.J., I can't risk you. You're everything that matters to me. I love you."

"And I'm supposed to sit here, like some helpless female, and risk you?"

"Exactly."

"You arrogant jerk. What am I supposed to do if you get yourself killed? In case you've forgotten, this is my problem, my deal. You're the one who's along for the ride, and you're not going anywhere without me."

"You'll be in my way."

"That's bull. I've held my own through this thing. I'm going, Jack, and unless you want to ride your thumb back to D.C., that's the deal."

He jerked away, snarling. Then whirled to pace. He considered cuffing her inside the house. It would be an ugly struggle—he could almost have looked forward to that aspect of it—and he'd win. But if things went wrong, he couldn't know how long it would be before someone found her.

No, he couldn't leave her alone and handcuffed in some isolated house in the boondocks.

He could lie. Agree to her terms, then ditch her. She wouldn't be easy to shake, but it was an option. Or he could try a different tack altogether.

He turned, smiled winningly. "Okay, sugar, I'll come clean. I've had enough."

"Have you?"

"It was fun. It was educational. But it's getting tedious. Even the fifty thousand you promised me just isn't worth risking my neck for. So I figured I'd cruise up north for a few weeks, wait for things to blow over.'' He gave a careless shrug as she stared at him. ''Things were getting a little heavy between you and me. That's not my style. So I figured I'd take off, avoid the obligatory scene. If I were you, I'd call the cops, turn over the stone, and chalk it all up to one of your more interesting holiday weekends.''

''You're dumping me,'' she said, in a small voice that made him feel like sludge.

''Let's say I'm just moving on. A guy's got to look out for number one.''

''All the things you said to me...''

''Hey, sugar, we're both free agents. We both know the score. Tell you what. I'll drop you off at the nearest town, give you a few bucks for transpo.''

In answer, she staggered toward the porch, every step a slice through his heart. When she collapsed, buried her face in her hands, he wished himself in hell.

She'll be safe, he reminded himself. All that mattered was that she'd be—

Laughing her guts out. He gaped as she threw back her head and roared with laughter. Her arms were clutched around her stomach, not in defense against heartbreak, but to keep herself from shaking apart with mirth.

''Oh, you idiot,'' she managed. ''Did you really think I was going to fall for that?'' She could hardly get the words out between great gusts of laughter. The darker his expression, the wilder her glee.

"Now, I guess, I'm supposed to tearfully hand over the distributor cap and let you leave me off somewhere to nurse my shattered heart." She wiped her streaming eyes. "You're so in love with me, Dakota, you can't think straight."

He was thinking straight enough, he determined. He wondered how she'd like it if he closed his hands over that throat of hers and gave it a nice, loving squeeze.

"I could get over it," he muttered.

"No, you couldn't. It's hit you right between the eyes, and I know the feeling. We're stuck with each other, Jack. There's no getting past it for either of us." She breathed deep, rubbed a hand over her aching ribs. "I ought to kick your butt for trying this, but it was too stupid. And too sweet."

He jammed his hands in his pockets. It was the "sweet" that made him feel most foolish. Outmaneuvering her hadn't worked, he considered. Temper and threats hadn't made a dent, and lies had only amused her.

So he would try the truth, he decided. Simple, unvarnished. And he would plead with it.

"Okay, you got me." He walked over, sat beside her, took her hand. "I've never told anyone I loved them before," he began. "I never loved anyone. Not a woman, not family, not a friend."

"Jack." Swamped with emotion, she brushed the hair from his brow. "You just never had a chance to."

"Doesn't matter." He said it fiercely, his fingers

tightening on hers. "I meant what I said last night. There's only you, M.J."

He pressed the back of her hand to his lips, held it there a moment. "You wouldn't understand that, not really. You've had other people in your life, important people."

"Yes." Touched, she leaned over, kissed his cheek. "There are people I love. Maybe there's not only you, Jack. But there is you. And what I feel for you is different than anything I've felt before, for anyone."

He stared down at their hands a moment. They fit so well, didn't they? he noticed. Just slid together, as if they'd been waiting for the match. "I've done things my own way for a long time," he continued. "I've avoided complications that I wasn't interested in. It's been easy to evade attachments. Until you."

He looked into her eyes as he touched a hand to her cheek. "You cried yesterday, over those other people you love. It cut me off at the knees. And when I was holding you, and you were crying, I knew I'd do anything for you. Let me do this."

"You planned to leave me here because I cried?"

"Because when you did I finally realized just what your friends mean to you, and how much you'd been holding it in. I need to help you. And them."

She looked away from him for a moment. It wouldn't do either of them any good if she wept again. And his words, and the quiet and deep emotion that flowed behind them, had touched her in a new part of her heart. "I already love you, Jack."

She let out a long sigh. "Now, I'm close to adoring you."

"Then you'll stay."

"No." She cupped his face as irritation raced over it. "But I'm not mad at you anymore."

"Great." He pushed off the steps to pace again. "Haven't you heard anything I've said? I can't risk you. I couldn't handle it if anything happened to you."

"But I'm supposed to handle it if something happens to you? It doesn't work that way, Jack." She rose and faced him. "Not for me. What you feel for me, I feel for you. We're in this together. Equal ground." She held up a hand before he could speak. "And you're not going to say something lame about you being a man and me being a woman."

Actually, it had been very close to coming out of his mouth. "A lot of good it would do me."

"Then it's settled." She angled her head. "And let me add something here, just in case you've got a bright idea about ditching me along the way. If you try it, I'll go to the nearest phone and call the cops. I'll tell them you kidnapped me, molested me. I'll give them your description, a description of what you call a car, and your tag number. You'll be trying to explain yourself to Sheriff Bubba and his team before you get twenty miles."

His eyes kindled. "You would, wouldn't you?"

"Damn straight. And I'll make it good, so good they'll probably mess up your pretty face before they toss you in a cell. Now, do we know where we stand?''

"Yeah." He pushed impotently against the corner she'd boxed him into. "We know where we stand. You cover your angles, sugar."

"You can count on that." She walked toward him, laid her hands on his tensed shoulders. "And you can count on me, Jack. I'm sticking with you." Expecting no response, she touched her lips to his. And got none. "I won't walk out on you," she murmured, and saw the flicker of understanding in his eyes. "And I won't let you down." She brushed her lips over his again. "I won't go away and leave you."

She saw too much, he realized. More, perhaps, than he'd seen himself. "This isn't about me."

"Yes, it is. No one's stuck with you, but I will. No one loved you enough, but I do." She skimmed her hands up his shoulders until they framed his face. "That makes all this about us. I'm going to be there for you, even when you try to play hero and shake me loose."

He was losing, and knew it. "You could start being there tomorrow."

"I'm already there. Now, are you going to kiss me, or not?"

"Maybe."

Her lips curved as they met his. Then they softened, and opened, and gave. He felt himself slide into her—a homecoming that was both sweet and exciting. The kiss heated even before she slipped her hands under his shirt, ran them up his back, then down again with nails scraping lightly.

"I want you," she murmured, moving sinuously against him. "Now, before we go—" she turned her head, nipped her teeth into his throat "—for luck."

His head swam as she reached between their bodies and found him. "I can always use a little extra luck."

She laughed, tugged him away from the car. They fell on the ground together and rolled over grass still damp with dew.

It was fast, and a little desperate. As the sun grew stronger, burning through the morning mist, they tugged at clothes, pawed each other.

"Let me..." He panted and dragged at denim. "I can't—"

"Here." Her hands fumbled with his, dragged material aside. "Hurry. God."

She rolled again, reared up and raced her mouth over his bare chest. She wanted to feast on him, needed to feast of those flavors, those textures. Sate herself with them. She would have sworn she felt the ground tremble as he turned her, hooked his teeth into her shoulder, one hand taking her breast, and the other...

"What are you... How can you..." Her head fell back as he ripped her viciously over the edge. Breath sobbing, she reached up, locked her arms around his neck and let the animal free.

She was with him, beat for beat, her body strong and agile. Her need was as greedy and as primal as his. Perhaps his hands bruised her in his rush, but hers were no less bold, no less rough. She turned her head, took his mouth with a wild avidity that tasted of the dark and the secret.

It was she who twisted, who dragged him down to her. "Now," she demanded, and her eyes gleamed like those of a cat on the hunt. "Right now." And wrapping herself around him, took him in.

He drove hard, burying himself in her. She met each rough, wild stroke, those tilted cat's eyes wide and focused on his. The heat of her fueled him, and through that edgy violence of need he felt his heart simply shatter with an emotion just as brutal.

"I love you." His mouth clamped on hers, drank from it. "God, I love you."

"I know." And when he pressed his face into her hair, shuddering as he poured himself into her, she needed to know nothing else.

"Jack." She stroked his hair. The sun was in her eyes, his weight was on her, and the grass was damp against her back. She thought it one of the finest moments of her life. "Jack," she said again, and sighed.

He nearly had his wind back. "Maybe there's something to country living after all." With a little groan, he propped up on his elbows. And felt his stomach sink. "What are you crying for? Are you trying to kill me?"

"I'm not. The sun's in my eyes." Then, feeling foolish, she flicked the single tear away. "It's not that kind of crying, anyway. Don't worry, I'm not going to blubber.''

"Did I hurt you? Look, I'm sorry, I—"

"Jack." She heaved another sigh. "It's not that kind of crying, okay? And I'm done now, anyway."

Wary, he studied those gleaming eyes. "Are you sure?"

"Yes." Then she smiled. "You coward."

"Guilty." And he wasn't ashamed to admit it. He kissed her nose. "Now that we've got all this extra luck, we'd better get going."

"You're not going to try to pull a fast one, are you?"

He thought of the way she'd taken his face in her hands and told him she was sticking. There had never been anyone in his life who ever made him that one simple promise.

"No. I guess we're a team."

"Good guess."

M.J. waited until they were back on the highway, heading toward civilization, before she asked. "Okay, Jack, what's the plan?"

"Nothing fancy. Simplicity has fewer pitfalls. The way I see it, we've got to get to whoever's pulling the strings. Our only link with him, or her, is the guys in the van and maybe the Salvinis."

"So far, I'm with you."

"I need to have a little chat with them. To do that, I have to lure them out, maintain the advantage and convince them it's in their best interest to pass on some information.''

"Okay, there are two guys with guns, one of whom is the approximate size of the Washington Monument. And you're going to convince them to chat with you." She beamed at him. "I admire your optimism.''

"It's all a matter of leverage," he said, and explained how he planned to accomplish it.

Thunder was rumbling in a darkened sky when he pulled up in the lot at Salvini. It was a dignified building, separated from a strip mall by a large parking lot. And it was locked tight for the Monday holiday.

In the smaller, well-tended Salvini lot sat a lone Mercedes sedan.

"Know who owns that?''

"One of the creeps—Bailey's stepbrothers. Thomas, I think. Bailey said they were closing down for an extended weekend. If he's inside, I don't know why.''

"Let's poke around.'' Jack got out, wandered to the sedan. It was locked tight, its security light blinking. He checked the front doors of the building first, scanned the darkened showroom, saw no signs of life.

"Offices upstairs?'' he asked M.J.

"Yeah. Bailey's, Thomas's, Timothy's.'' Her heart began to race. "Maybe she's in there, Jack. She rarely drives to work. We live so close.''

"Uh-huh." And though it wasn't part of his plan, the worry in her voice had him going with impulse and pressing the buzzer beside the door. "Let's check the rear," he said a moment later.

"They could be holding her inside. She could be hurt. I should have thought of it before." Toward the west, lightning forked down like jagged blades. "She could be in there, hurt and—"

He turned. "Listen, if we're going to get through this, you've got to hold it together. We don't have time for a lot of hand-wringing and speculation."

Her head jerked back, then she squared her shoulders. "All right. Sorry."

After a short study of her face, he nodded, then continued to the back, where he took a long look at the steel security door. "Someone's been at the locks."

"What do you mean, 'at'?" She leaned over his shoulder as he crouched down. "Do you mean someone picked the locks?"

"Fairly recently, no rust, no dust in the scrapes. Wonder if he got in." He rose, examined the sides, the jambs. "He didn't try to jimmy it or hammer against it. I'd say he knew what he was doing. Under different circumstances, I'd say it was just your average break-in, but that's stretching it."

"Can you get in?"

That wasn't part of the immediate plan, either, but he considered. "Probably. Do you know what kind of alarm system they've got?"

"There's a box inside the door. It's coded. I don't

know the code. You punch some numbers.'' She caught herself before she could indeed wring her hands. ''Jack.'' She struggled to keep her voice calm. ''She could be in there. She could be hurt. If we don't check, and something goes wrong…''

''Okay. But if I can't deal with the alarm, and fast, we're going to get busted.'' Still, he got his tools out of the trunk and went to work.

''Watch my back, will you?'' he told her. ''Make sure none of those holiday shoppers next door take an interest over here.''

She turned, scanned the lot and the strip mall beyond. People came and went, obviously too involved in the bargains they'd bagged or those they were hunting to take notice of a man crouched at a security door of a locked building.

Thunder walked closer, and rain, long awaited, began to flood out of the sky. She didn't mind getting wet, considered the storm only a better cover. But she shuddered with relief when he gave her the all-clear.

''Once I open this, I've probably got a minute to ninety seconds before the alarm. If I can't disengage it, we'll have to go, and fast.''

''But—''

''No arguments here, M.J. If, by any chance, Bailey's in there, the cops'll be along in minutes, and they'll find her. We'll take our show on the road elsewhere. Agreed?''

What choice was there? ''Agreed.''

''Fine.'' He swiped dripping hair out of his eyes.

"You stay right here. If I say go, you head for the car." Taking her silence for assent, he stepped inside. He saw the alarm box immediately, lifted a brow. "Interesting," he murmured, then signaled M.J. inside. "It's off."

"I don't understand that. It's always set."

"Just our lucky day." He winked, took her hand, then flipped on his flashlight with the other. "We'll try upstairs first, see if we get lucky again."

"Up these stairs," she told him. "Bailey's office is right down the hall."

"Nice digs," he commented, scanning the expensive carpeting, the tasteful colors, while keeping his ears tuned for any sound. There was nothing but drumming rain. He blocked M.J. with an outstretched arm, and swept the light into the office.

Quiet, organized, elegant and empty. He heard M.J. let out a rusty breath.

"No sign of struggle," he pointed out. "We'll check the rest of the floor, then downstairs before we go into phase one of plan A."

He moved down the hall and, a full yard before the next door, stopped. "Go back in her office, wait for me."

"Why? What is it?" Then she caught the heaviness in the air, recognized it for what it was. "Bailey! Oh, my God."

Jack rapped her back against the wall, pinned her until her struggles ceased. "You do what I tell you," he said between his teeth. "You stay here."

She closed her eyes, admitted there were some things she wasn't strong enough to face. Nodded.

Satisfied, he eased back. He moved down the hall quietly, eased the door open.

It was as bad as he'd ever seen, and death was rarely pretty. But this, he thought, trailing the light over the wreckage caused by a life-and-death struggle, had been madness.

Life had lost.

He turned away from it, went back to M.J. She was pale as wax, leaning against the wall. "It's not Bailey," he said immediately. "It's a man."

"Not Bailey?"

"No." He put a hand to her cheek, found it icy, but her eyes were losing their glazed look. "I'm going to check the other rooms. I don't want you to go in there, M.J."

She let out the breath that had been hot and trapped in her lungs. Not Bailey. "Was it like Ralph?"

"No." His voice was flat and hard. "It was a hell of a lot worse. Stay here."

He went through each room, checked corners and closets, careful not to touch anything or to wipe a surface when he had no choice but to touch. Saying nothing, he led M.J. downstairs and did a quick, thorough search of the lower level.

"Someone's been in here," he murmured, hunkering down to shine the light into a tiny alcove under the stairs. "The dust's disturbed." Considering, he stroked his chin. "I'd say if somebody was smart and needed a bolt hole, this would be a good choice.''

Her clothes were clinging wet against her skin. But that wasn't why she was shivering. ''Bailey's smart.''

He nodded, rose. ''Keep that in mind. Let's do what we came for.''

''Okay.'' She cast one last look over her shoulder, imagined Bailey hiding in the dark. From what? she wondered. From whom? And where was she now?

Outside, Jack secured the door, wiped the knob. ''I figure if you need to, you can get over to that mall on those legs of yours in about thirty seconds at a sprint.''

''I'm not running away.''

''You will if I tell you.'' He pocketed the flashlight. ''You're going to do exactly what I tell you. No questions, no arguments, no hesitation.'' His eyes flared into hers, made her shiver again. ''Whoever did what I found upstairs is an animal. You remember that.''

''I will.'' She clamped down ruthlessly on the next tremor. ''And you remember we're in this together.''

''The idea is for me to take these guys down, one at a time. If you can get to the van while I'm distracting them and disable it, fine. But don't take any chances.''

''I've already told you I wouldn't.''

''Once I have them secured,'' he continued, ignoring the impatience in her voice, ''we can use their van. I can have a nice chat with them. I think I can get a name out of them.'' He examined his fist, then smiled craftily over it into her eyes. "Some basic information.''

"Oooh...'' She fluttered her wet lashes. "So macho.''

"Shut up. Depending on the name and information we get, and the situation, we either go to the cops—which would be my second choice—or we follow the next lead.''

"Agreed.''

He opened the door of his car, waited until she slid over the seat, then picked up her phone. "Make the call. Stretch it out for about a minute, just in case.''

She dialed, then began to ramble to Grace's answering machine in Potomac. She kept her eyes on Jack's, and when he nodded, she pushed disconnect. "Phase two?" she said, struggling for calm.

"Now we wait.''

Within fifteen minutes, the van turned into the lot at Salvini. The rain had slowed now, but continued to fall in a steady stream. In his position beside an aging station wagon, Jack hunched his shoulders against the wet and watched the routine.

The two men got out, separated and did a slow circle of the building.

The big one was his target.

Using parked cars as cover, Jack made his way over, watching as the man bent, picked up M.J.'s phone from the ground. It was a decent plant, Jack mused, gave him something to consider in that pea-size brain of his. As the big man pondered over the phone, Jack sprang and hit him at a dead run, bashing into his kidneys like a cannonball.

He took his quarry to his knees, and had the cuffs snapped over one steel-beam wrist before he was flicked off like a fly.

He felt the searing burn as his flesh scraped over wet, grainy asphalt, and rolled before a size-sixteen shoe could bash into his face. He made the grab, snagged the sledgehammer of a foot and heaved.

From her post, M.J. watched the struggle, wincing as Jack hit the ground, praying as he rolled. Hissing as fists crunched against bone. She started quietly toward the van, glancing back to see the progress of the bout.

He was outmatched, she thought desperately. Was going to get his neck broken, at the very least. Braced to spring to his aid, she saw the second man rounding the far corner of the building.

He'd be on them in moments, she thought. And Jack's plan to take them both quickly and separately was in tatters. She sucked in the breath to call out a warning, then narrowed her eyes. Maybe there was still a way to make it work.

She dashed out from behind cover, took a short run toward Salvini, away from Jack. She skidded to a halt when she saw the second man spot her, made her eyes widen with shock and fear. His hand went inside his jacket, but she held fast, waiting until he began closing in.

Then she ran, into the curtaining rain, drawing him away from Jack.

Both Jack and his sparring partner heard the shout. Both looked over instinctively and saw the woman with the bright cap of red hair racing away, and the man pursuing her.

Never listens, Jack thought with a bright spear of terror. Then he looked back, saw the big man grinning at him.

Jack grinned back, and his swollen left eye gleamed bright with malice. "Gotta take you down, and fast," he said conversationally as he rammed a fist into the man's mouth. "That's my woman your pal's chasing."

The giant swiped blood from his face. "You're meat."

"Yeah?" There wasn't any time to dally. Praying M.J.'s legs and his neck would hold out, he lowered his head and charged like a mad bull. The force of the attack shot the man back, rapping his head smartly on the steel door. Bloodied, battered and exhausted, Jack drove his knee up, hard and high, and heard the satisfactory sound of air gushing out of a deflated blimp.

Blinking stinging sweat and warm rain out of his eyes, Jack wrenched the man's arms back, snapped on the second cuff.

"I'll be back for you," he promised, as he retrieved the phone and tore off in search of M.J.

Chapter 12

Jack had told her, if anything went wrong, to head for the shops, to lose herself in the crowds. Scream bloody murder if necessary.

With that on her mind, M.J. veered that way, her priority to lure the second gunman away from Jack and give him an even chance.

But as she raced toward the stores, with their bright On Sale signs, she saw couples, families, children being led by the hand, babies in strollers. And thought of the way the man chasing her had slipped a hand under his jacket.

She thought of what a gun fired at her in the midst of a crowd would do.

And she pivoted, changed direction on a dime and ran toward the far end of the lot.

Pumping her arms, she tossed a quick look over

her shoulder. She'd left her pursuer in the dust. He was still coming, but lagging now, overheated, she imagined, in his bagging suit coat and leather shoes. Slippery shoes on wet pavement. Just how far would he chase her, she wondered, before giving up and turning back to pick up his friend?

And stumble over Jack.

Deliberately she slowed her pace, let him close some of the distance, in order to keep his interest keen. Part of her worried that he would simply use that gun, slam a bullet into her leg. Or her back. With the image of that running riot in her head, she streaked into a line of parked cars.

She could hear her own breath whistling now. She'd run the equivalent of a fifty-yard touchdown dash in the blistering heat of a midsummer storm. Crouching behind a minivan, she swiped sweat from her eyes and tried to think.

Could she circle back, find a way to help Jack? Had the gorilla already pounded him into dust and set off to help his buddy? How long would her luck last before some innocent family of four, their bargain-hunting complete, ran through the downpour and into the line of fire?

Concentrating on silence more than speed, she duckwalked around the van, slid her way around a compact. She needed to catch her breath, needed to think. Needed to see what was happening behind the Salvini building.

Bracing herself, she put one trembling hand on the fender of the compact and risked a quick look.

He was closer than she'd anticipated. Four cars to the left, and taking his time. She ducked down fast, pressed her back into the bumper. If she stayed where she was, would he pass by, or would he spot her?

Better to die on the run, she thought, or with your fists raised, than to be picked off cowering behind an economy import.

She sucked in a breath, said another quick prayer for Jack, and headed for new ground. It was the ping on the asphalt beside her that stopped her heart. She felt the sharp edge of rock bounce off her jeans.

He was shooting at her. Her heart bounced from throat to stomach and back like a Ping-Pong ball, and she skidded around a parked car. Another inch, two at the most, and that bullet would have met flesh.

He'd tagged her, she realized. And now it would only be a matter of running her down, cornering her like a rabbit. Well, she would see about that.

Gritting her teeth, she bellied under the car, ignored the wet grit, the smell of gas and oil, and slid like a snake beneath the undercarriage, held her breath as she pulled herself through the narrow space and under the next vehicle.

She could hear him now. He was breathing hard, a wheeze on each inhale, a whistle on the exhale. She saw his shoes. Little feet, she thought irreverently, decked out in glossy black wing tips and argyle socks.

She closed her eyes for one brief moment, trying to get a picture of him planted in her mind. Five-eight, tops, maybe a hundred and sixty. Mid-thirties.

Sharp eyes, a well-defined nose. Wiry but not buff. And out of breath.

Hell, she thought, going giddy. She could take him.

She scooted another inch, was just preparing to make her move when she saw those shiny wing tips leave the ground.

There in front of her eyes were a pair of scuffed boots. Jack's boots. Jack's voice was muttering panting curses. Her vision blurred with relief and the terror as she heard the muffled thump that was the silenced gun firing again.

Skinning elbows and knees, she was out from under the car in time to see the gunman running for cover and Jack starting off in pursuit.

"Jack."

He skidded to a halt, whirled, sheer relief covering his battered face. And it was then that she saw the blood staining his shirt.

"Oh, God. Oh, God. You're shot." Her legs went weak, so that she stumbled toward him as he glanced down absently, pressing a hand to his side.

"Hell." The pain registered, but only dimly, as his arms filled with woman. "The car," he managed. "Get to the car. He's heading back."

His hand, wet with blood and rain, locked on hers.

Later, she would remember running. But none of it seemed real as it happened. Feet pounding on pavement, skidding, the jittery thud of her heart, the rising sense of fear and fury, the wide, shocked eyes of a woman carrying shopping bags who was nearly mowed down in their rush.

And Jack cursing her, steadily, for not doing as she was told.

The van screamed out of the lot as they skidded down the incline. "Damn it all to hell and back again." His lungs were burning, his side shot fire. Desperately he dug the keys out of his pocket. "In the car. Now!"

She all but dived through the window, barely maintaining her balance as he burned rubber in reverse. "You're hurt. Let me see—"

He batted her worried hands away and whipped the wheel around. "He got his three-ton friend, too. After all that trouble, they're not getting away." The car shimmied, fishtailed, then the tires bit the road as he swung into the chase. "Get the gun out of the glove box. Give it to me."

"Jack, you're bleeding. For God's sake."

"Didn't I tell you to run?" He punched the gas, screaming on the van's rear bumper as they rocketed toward the main drag. "I told you to head for people, to get lost. He could have killed you. Give me the damn gun."

"All right, all right." She beat a fist on the glove compartment until the sticky door popped open. "He's heading for the Beltway."

"I see where he's going."

"You're not going to shoot at him. You could hit some poor schmuck's car."

Jack snatched the gun out of her hand, swerved to

make the exit, skidded on the damp roadway. "I hit what I aim at. Now strap in and be quiet. I'll deal with you later."

Her fear for him was such that she didn't blink an eye at his words. He zipped through traffic like a madman, hugging the bumper of the van like a lover. And when they hit ninety, a cold numbness settled over her, as if her system had been shot full of novocaine.

"You're going to kill someone," she said calmly. "It might not even be us."

"I can handle the car." That, at least, was perfect truth. He threaded through traffic, staying on target like a heat-seeking missile, his fat new tires gripping true on the slick roadway. He was close enough that he could see the big man hunched in the passenger seat turn around and snarl.

"Yeah, I'm coming for you, you son of a bitch," Jack muttered. "You've got my spare cuffs."

"You're bleeding on the seat." M.J. heard herself speak, but the words seemed to come from outside her mind.

"I've got more." And with the gun on his lap, he whipped the wheel, gained inches on the side. He'd cut them off, he calculated, drive them to the shoulder. The big man was cuffed, and he could handle the other.

And then, they would see.

His eyes narrowed as he saw the driver of the van twist his head around, heard the wheels screech. The van shimmied, shuddered, then swerved wildly toward the oncoming exit.

"He can't make it." Jack pumped his brakes, fell back a foot and prepared to make the quick, sharp turn. "He can't make that turn. He'll lose it."

He swore when the van rocked, lost control on the rain-slicked road and hit the guardrail at eighty. The crash was huge, and sent the van flying up like a drunken high diver. It rolled once in the air. And amid the squeal of brakes of other horrified drivers, it landed twelve feet below, on the incline.

He had time to swing to the side, to push out of the car, before the explosion shoved him back like a huge, hot hand. M.J.'s hand gripped his shoulder as the flames spewed up. The air stank with gas.

"Not a chance," he murmured. "Lost them."

"Get in the car, Jack." It amazed her how cool, how composed, her voice sounded. Cars were emptying of drivers and passengers. People were rushing toward the wreck. "In the passenger side. I'm driving now."

"After all that," he said, dazed with smoke and pain. "Lost them anyway."

"In the car." She led him around, ignoring the high, excited voices. Someone, surely, would have already called 911 on his car phone. There was nothing left to do. "We need to get out of here."

She drove on instinct back to her apartment. Safe or not, it was home, and he needed tending. Driving Jack's car was like manning a yacht, she thought, concentrating on her speed and direction as the rain petered out to a fine drizzle. A very old, very big boat. With a vague sense of surprise, she pulled in beside her MG.

Nothing much had changed, she realized. Her car was still there, the building still stood. A couple of kids who didn't mind getting wet were tossing a Frisbee in the side yard, as if it was an ordinary day in ordinary lives.

"Wait for me to come around." She dragged up her purse from the floor, found her keys. Of course, he didn't listen, and was standing on the sidewalk when she came around the hood. "You can lean on me," she murmured, sliding an arm around his waist. "Just lean on me, Jack."

"It should be all right to be here," he decided. "At least for a little while. We may have to move again soon." He realized he was limping, favoring an ache in his right leg that he hadn't noticed before.

Her heart had stopped stuttering and was numb. "We'll just get you cleaned up."

"Yeah. I could use a beer."

"I'll get you one," she promised as she led him inside. Though she habitually took the stairs, she steered him to the elevator. "Let's just get you inside." And then to a hospital, she thought. She had to see how bad it was first. Once she'd done what she could, she was dumping it all and going official. Cops, doctors, FBI, whatever it took.

She sent up a small prayer of thanksgiving when she saw that the corridor was empty. No nosy neighbors, she thought, ignoring the police tape and unlocking her door. No awkward questions.

She kicked a broken lamp out of her way, walked him around the overturned couch and into the bath. "Sit," she ordered, and flicked on the lights. "Let's have a look." And her trembling hands belied her steady voice as she gently lifted his bloody shirt over his head.

"God, Jack, that guy beat the hell out of you."

"I left him with his face in the dirt and his hands cuffed behind his back."

"Yeah." She made herself look away from the blooming purple bruises over his torso and wet a cloth. "Have you been shot before?"

"Once, in Abilene. Caught me in the leg. Slowed me down awhile."

Ridiculous as it was, it helped that this wasn't the first time. She pressed the cloth to his side, low along the ribs. Her eyes stung with hot tears that she wouldn't shed. "I know it hurts."

"You were going to get me a beer." Didn't she look pretty, he thought, playing nurse, with her cheeks pale, her eyes dark, and her hands cool as silk.

"In a minute. Just be still now." She knelt beside him, steeling herself for the worst. Then sat back on her heels and hissed. "Damn it, Jack, it's only a scratch."

He grinned at her, feeling every bump and bruise as if in a personal carnival of pain. "That's supposed to be my line."

"I was ready for some big gaping hole in your side. It just grazed you."

He looked down, considered. "Bled pretty good, though." He took the cloth himself, pressed it against the long, shallow wound. "About that beer..."

"I'll get you a beer. I ought to hit you over the head with it."

"We'll talk about who conks who after I eat a bottle of aspirin." He got up, wincing, and pawed through the mirrored cabinet over the sink. "Maybe you could get me a shirt out of the car, sugar. I don't think I'm going to be wearing the other one again."

"You scared me." Anger, tears and desperate relief brewed a messy stew in her stomach. "Do you have any idea how much you scared me?"

He found the aspirin, closed the cabinet and met her eyes in the mirror. "I've got an idea, seeing how I felt when I saw you trying to draw that puss-for-brain's fire. You promised to head for the mall."

"Well, I didn't. Sue me." Out of patience, she shoved him down again, ignoring his muffled yelp of pain. "Oh, be quiet and let me finish up here. I must have some antiseptic here somewhere."

"Maybe just a leather strap to bite on while you pour salt in my wounds."

"Don't tempt me." She dampened another cloth, then knelt down and began to clean his face. "You've got a black eye blooming, your lip's swollen, and you've got a nice big knot right here." He yelped again when she pressed the cloth to his temple. "Baby."

"If you're going to play Nurse Nancy, at least give me some anesthesia first." Since she didn't seem inclined to give him any water, he swallowed the aspirin dry.

He continued to complain as she swabbed him with antiseptic, slapped on bandages. Out of patience, she pressed her lips to his, which caused him equal amounts of pain and pleasure. "Are you going to kiss everywhere it hurts?" he asked.

"You should be so lucky." Then she laid her head in his lap and let out a long, long sigh. "I don't care how mad you are. I didn't know what else to do. He was coming. He'd have had you. I only knew I had to draw him away from you."

He weakened, stroked her hair. "Okay, we'll get into all that later." He noticed for the first time the raw skin on her elbow. "Hey, you've got a few scrapes yourself."

"Burns some," she murmured.

"Aw. Come on, sugar, I'll be the doctor." He reversed their positions, grinned. "This may sting a little."

"You'd love that, wouldn't— Ouch! Damn it, Jack."

"Baby." But he kissed the abraded skin, then bandaged it gently. "You ever scare me like that again, and I'll keep you cuffed to the bed for a month."

"Promises, promises." She leaned forward, wrapped her arms around him. "They're dead, aren't they? They couldn't have lived through that."

"Chances are slim. I'm sorry, M.J., I never got anything out of them. Not a clue."

"*We* never got anything out of them," she corrected. "And we did our best." She struggled to bury the worry, straighten her shoulders. "There's still the creeps," she began, then went pale again, remembering. Odds were at least one of the Salvini brothers was dead.

But it hadn't been Bailey in there, she reminded herself, and took two deep breaths. "Well, at least now I can get myself some fresh clothes and some cash. And I'm calling into the pub." This was a dare. "I'll wait until we're ready to head out again, but I'm checking in, letting them know I'm okay, giving them the schedule for the rest of the week."

"Fine, be a businesswoman." He stood up, held her still. "We'll find your friends, M.J. I promise you that. And as much as it goes against the grain, it's time to call in the cops."

She let out a wavering sigh of relief. "Yeah. Three days of this is enough."

"There'll be a lot of questions."

"Then we'll give them the answers."

"I should tell you that a man in my line of work isn't real popular with straight cops. I've got a couple of contacts, but when you start moving up the ranks, the tolerance level shoots way down."

"We'll handle it. Should we call from here, or just go in?"

"Here. Cop shops make me itchy."

"I'm not giving them the stone." She planted her

feet, prepared for an argument. "It's Bailey's—or it's her decision. I'm not turning it over to anyone but her."

"Okay," he said easily, and made her blink. "We'll work around it. She and Grace come first, with both of us now."

Her smile spread. And the jangling ring made them both jolt. "What?" She stared down at her purse as if it had suddenly come alive and snapped at her. "It's my phone. My phone's ringing."

He touched a hand to his pocket, reassured when he felt the gun. "Answer it."

Barely breathing, she dug into the purse she'd dropped on the floor, hit the switch. "O'Leary." The tears simply rushed into her eyes as she sank down on the floor. "Bailey. Oh, my God, Bailey. Are you all right? Where are you? Are you hurt? What—What? Yes, yes, I'm fine. In my apartment, but where—"

Her hand reached up, gripped Jack's. "Bailey, stop asking me that and tell me where the hell you are. Yeah, I've got it. We'll be there in ten minutes. Stay."

She clicked off. "I'm sorry," she told Jack. "I've got to." Then burst into tears. "She's all right," she managed as he rolled his eyes and picked her up. "She's okay."

It was a quiet, established neighborhood with lovely old trees. M.J. gripped her hands together on her lap and scanned house numbers. "Twenty-two,

twenty-four, twenty-six. There! That one.'' Even as
Jack turned into the driveway of a tidy Federal-style
home, she was reaching for the door handle. He
merely hooked a hand in the waist of her jeans and
hauled her back.

"Hold on, wait until I stop."

Even as he did, he saw the woman, a pretty blonde
of fragile build, come racing out of the front door
and across the wet grass. M.J. shoved herself out of
the car and streaked into her arms.

It made a nice picture, Jack decided as he climbed
out, gingerly. The two of them standing in the watery
sunlight, holding on as if they could swallow each
other whole. They swayed together on the lush grass,
weeping, talking over each other and just clinging.

And as touching and attractive a scene as it was,
there was nothing he wanted to avoid more than two
sobbing women. He spotted the man standing just
outside the door, noted the smile in his eyes, the fresh
bandage on his arm. Without hesitation, Jack gave
the women a wide berth and headed for the front
door.

"Cade Parris."

Jack took the extended hand, measured his man.
About six-two, trim, brown hair, eyes of a dreamier
green than M.J.'s. A strong grip that Jack felt balanced out the glossy good looks.

"Jack Dakota."

Cade scanned the bruises, shook his head. "You
look like a man who could use a drink."

Despite his sore mouth, Jack's lips spread in a

grateful smile. "Brother, you just became my best friend."

"Come on in," Cade invited, with a last glance toward M.J. and Bailey. "They'll need some time, and we can fill each other in."

It took a while, but Jack was feeling considerably more relaxed, with his feet propped up on a coffee table, a beer in his hand.

"Amnesia," he murmured. "Must have been tough on her."

"She's had a rough few days. Seeing one slimy excuse for a stepbrother kill her other slimy excuse for a stepbrother, then come for her."

"We dropped in on Salvini's. I saw the results."

Cade nodded. "Then you know how bad it was. If she hadn't gotten away... Well, she did. She still doesn't remember all of it, but she'd already sent one of the diamonds to M.J. and one to Grace. I've been working the case since Friday morning, when she came to my office. You?"

"Saturday afternoon," Jack told him and cooled his throat with beer.

"It's been fast work all around." But Cade frowned as he looked toward the window. "Bailey was scared, confused, but she wanted answers and figured a private investigator could get them for her. We had a major breakthrough today."

Jack lifted a brow, gesturing toward the bandage. "That part of it?"

"The remaining Salvini," Cade said, his eyes level and cold. "He's dead."

Which meant one more dead end, Jack mused. "You figure they set the whole thing up?"

"No. They had a client. I haven't tracked him yet." Cade rose, wandered to the window. M.J. and Bailey were still standing in the yard, talking fast. "Cops are on it too, now. I've got a friend. Mick Marshall."

"Yeah, I know him. He's a rare one. A cop with a brain and a heart."

"That's Mick. Buchanan's over him, though. He doesn't much like P.I.'s."

"Buchanan doesn't much like anybody. But he's good."

"He's going to want to talk to you, and M.J."

The prospect had Jack sighing. "I think I could use another beer."

With a laugh, Cade turned from the window. "I'll get us both another. And you can tell me how you spent your weekend." His eyes roamed over Jack's face. "And how the other guy looks."

"Timothy," M.J. said with surprise. "I never liked him, but I never pictured him as a murderer."

"It was as if he'd lost his mind." Bailey kept her hand linked with M.J.'s, as if afraid her friend would vanish without the connection. "I blanked it all, just shut it out. Everything. Little pieces started to come back, but I couldn't get a grip on them. I wouldn't have made it through without Cade."

"I can't wait to meet him." She looked into Bailey's eyes, and her own narrowed in speculation. "It looks as though he works fast."

"It shows?" Bailey asked, and flushed.

"Like a big neon sign."

"Just days ago," Bailey said, half to herself. "It all happened fast. It doesn't seem like just a few days. It feels as if I've known him forever." Her lips curved, warmed her honey-brown eyes. "He loves me, M.J. Just like that. I know it sounds crazy."

"You'd be surprised what doesn't sound crazy to me these days. He makes you happy?" M.J. tucked Bailey's wave of hair behind her ear. "That's what counts."

"I couldn't remember you. Or Grace." A tear squeezed through as Bailey shut her eyes. "I know it was only a couple of days, but it was so lonely without you. Then, when I started to remember, it wasn't specifics, more just a feeling. A loss of something important. Then, when I did remember, and we went to your apartment, you were gone. There'd been the break-in, and I couldn't find you. Everything happened so fast after that. It was only hours ago. Then I remembered that phone you cart around in your purse. I remembered and I called. And there you were."

"It was the best call I ever got."

"The best I ever made." Her lips trembled once. "M.J., I can't find Grace."

"I know." Drawing together, M.J. draped an arm around Bailey's shoulders. "We have to believe she's all right. Jack and I were just up at her country place this morning. She'd been there, Bailey. I could still smell her. And we found each other. We'll find her.''

"Yes, we will.'' They walked toward the house together. "This Jack? Does he make you happy?''

"Yeah. When he's not ticking me off.''

With a chuckle, Bailey opened the door. "Then I can't wait to meet him, either.''

"I like your friend.'' Jack stood out on Cade's patio, contemplating after-the-rain in suburbia.

"She likes you, too.''

"She's classy. And she's come through a rough time holding her own. Parris seems pretty sharp.''

"He helped get her through, so he's aces with me.''

"We filled in most of the blanks for each other. He's got a cool head, a quick mind. And he's crazy about your friend.''

"I think I noticed that.''

Jack took her hand, studied it. Not delicate like Bailey's, he mused, but narrow, competent. Strong. "He's got a lot to offer. Class again, money, fancy house. I guess you'd call it security.''

Intrigued, she watched his face. "I guess you would.''

He hadn't meant to get started on this, he realized. But however fast certain things could move, he'd decided life was too short to waste time.

"My old man was a bum,'' he said abruptly. "My

mother served drinks to drunks when she felt like working. I worked my way thorough college hauling bricks and mixing mortar for a mason, which led me to a useless degree in English lit with a minor in anthropology. Don't ask me why, it seemed like the thing to do at the time. I've got a few thousand socked away for dry spells. You get dry spells in my line of work. I rent a couple of rooms by the month.''

He waited a beat, but she said nothing. "Not what you'd call security.''

"Nope.''

"Is that what you want? Security?''

She thought about it. "Nope.''

He dragged his hand through his hair. "You know how those two stones looked when you and Bailey put them together? They looked spectacular, sure, all that fire and power in one spot. But mostly, they just looked right.'' He met her eyes, tried to see inside her. "Sometimes, it's just right.''

"And when it is, you don't have to look for the reasons.''

"Maybe not. I don't know what I'm doing here. I don't know why this is. I've lived my life alone, and liked it that way. Do you understand that?''

She enjoyed the irritation in his voice, and smirked. "Yeah, I understand that. The lone wolf. You want to howl at the moon tonight, or what?''

"Don't get smart with me when I'm trying to explain myself.''

He took a quick circle around the patio. There was a hammock swinging between two big trees, and somewhere in those dripping green leaves a bird was singing its heart out.

His life, Jack mused, had never been that simple, that calm, or that pretty. He didn't have anything to offer but what he was, and what he had inside himself for her.

She'd have to decide if that was enough to build on.

"The point is, I don't want to keep living my life alone." His head snapped up, and his bruised eye glared out from under the arched, scarred brow. "Do you understand that?"

"Why wouldn't I?" Her smirk remained firmly in place. "You're sloppy in love with me, pal."

"Keep it up, just keep it up." He hissed out a breath, eased a hand onto his aching side. "My feelings aren't the issue, and maybe yours aren't, either. Things happen to people's emotions under intense circumstances."

"Now he's being philosophical again. Must be that minor in anthropology."

He closed his eyes, prayed for patience. "I'm trying to lay out my cards here. You come from a different place than I do, and maybe you don't want to head where I'm heading. Maybe you want to slow down some now, take it in more careful steps. More traditional."

Now she snorted. "Is that how I strike you? The traditional type?"

His frown only deepened. "Maybe not, but it doesn't change the fact that a week ago you were cruising along in your own lane just fine. You've got a right to ask questions, look for reasons. A couple of days with me—''

"I'm not asking questions or looking for reasons, Jack," she said, interrupting him. "I stopped cruising in my own lane the day I met you, and I'm glad of it."

Oh, hell, she thought, and braced. "It stands for Magdalen Juliette."

A cough of laughter escaped him. It was the last thing he'd expected. "You're kidding."

"It stands for Magdalen Juliette," she repeated between clenched teeth. "And the only people who know that are my family, Bailey and Grace. In other words, only people I love and trust, which now includes you."

"Magdalen Juliette," he repeated, rolling it around on his tongue. "Quite a handle, sugar."

"It's M.J. Legally M.J., because that's what I wanted. And if you ever call me any form of Magdalen Juliette other than M.J., I will personally and with great pleasure skin you alive."

She would, too, he thought with a quick, crooked grin. "If you don't want me using it, why did you tell me?"

She took a step toward him. "I told you that, and I'm telling you this, because my name is M. J. O'Leary, and I know what I want."

His eyes flared and burned away the grin. "You're sure of that?"

"The second stone's knowledge. And I know. Do you?"

"Yeah." His breathing took a hitch. "It's a big step."

"The biggest."

"Okay." His palms were sweaty in his pockets, so he pulled them free. "You go first."

Her grin flashed. "No, you."

"No way. I said it first last time. Fair's fair."

She supposed it was. Angling her head, she took a good long look at him. Yes, she thought. She knew. "Okay. Let's get married."

Relishing the swift kick of joy, he tucked his thumbs in his pockets. "Aren't you supposed to ask? You know, propose? A guy's entitled to a little romance at big moments."

"You're pushing your luck." Then she laughed and locked her arms around his neck. "But what the hell—will you marry me, Jack?"

"Sure, why not?"

And when she laughed again, he caught her against his sore and battered body.

Perfect fit.

* * * * *

Take 4 bestselling love stories FREE

Plus get a FREE surprise gift!

Return to the Towers!

In March
New York Times bestselling author

NORA ROBERTS

brings us to the Calhouns' fabulous
Maine coast mansion and reveals the
tragic secrets hidden there for generations.

For all his degrees, Professor Max Quartermain has a
lot to learn about love—and luscious Lilah Calhoun is
just the woman to teach him. Ex-cop Holt Bradford is
as prickly as a thornbush—until Suzanna Calhoun's
special touch makes love blossom in his heart.
And all of them are caught in the race to solve
the generations-old mystery of a priceless
lost necklace...and a timeless love.

Lilah and Suzanna
THE
Calhoun Women

**A special 2-in-1 edition containing
FOR THE LOVE OF LILAH and
SUZANNA'S SURRENDER**

Available at your favorite retail outlet.

As seen on TV!
Free Gift Offer

With a Free Gift proof-of-purchase from any Silhouette® book,
you can receive a beautiful cubic zirconia pendant.

This gorgeous marquise-shaped stone is a genuine cubic
zirconia—accented by an 18" gold tone necklace.

(Approximate retail value $19.95)

Send for yours today...

compliments of ▼ *Silhouette*®
TM

To receive your free gift, a cubic zirconia pendant, send us one original proof-of-purchase, photocopies not accepted, from the back of any Silhouette Romance™, Silhouette Desire®, Silhouette Special Edition®, Silhouette Intimate Moments® or Silhouette Yours Truly™ title available at your favorite retail outlet, together with the Free Gift Certificate, plus a check or money order for $1.65 U.S./$2.15 CAN. (do not send cash) to cover postage and handling, payable to Silhouette Free Gift Offer. We will send you the specified gift. Allow 6 to 8 weeks for delivery. Offer good until December 31, 1997, or while quantities last. Offer valid in the U.S. and Canada only.

Free Gift Certificate

Name: _____

Address: _____

City: _____ State/Province: _____ Zip/Postal Code: _____

Mail this certificate, one proof-of-purchase and a check or money order for postage and handling to: SILHOUETTE FREE GIFT OFFER 1997. In the U.S.: 3010 Walden Avenue, P.O. Box 9077, Buffalo NY 14269-9077. In Canada: P.O. Box 613, Fort Erie, Ontario L2Z 5X3.

FREE GIFT OFFER   084-KFD

ONE PROOF-OF-PURCHASE
To collect your fabulous FREE GIFT, a cubic zirconia pendant, you must include this
original proof-of-purchase for each gift with the properly completed Free Gift Certificate.

084-KFDR

CHRISTINE FLYNN

**Continues the twelve-book
series—36 HOURS—in
December 1997 with
Book Six**

FATHER AND CHILD REUNION

Eve Stuart was back, and Rio Redtree couldn't ignore the fact
that her daughter bore his Native American features. So, Eve
had broken his heart *and* kept him from his child! But this
was no time for grudges, because his little girl and her
mother, the woman he had never stopped—could never stop—
loving, were in danger, and Rio would stop at nothing to
protect *his* family.

For Rio and Eve and *all* the residents of Grand Springs,
Colorado, the storm-induced blackout was just the beginning
of 36 Hours that changed *everything!* You won't want to
miss a single book.

Available at your favorite retail outlet.

Look us up on-line at: http://www.romance.net   36HRS6

SILHOUETTE WOMEN KNOW ROMANCE WHEN THEY SEE IT.

And they'll see it on **ROMANCE CLASSICS**, the new 24-hour TV channel devoted to romantic movies and original programs like the special **Romantically Speaking—Harlequin™ Goes Prime Time**.

Romantically Speaking—Harlequin™ Goes Prime Time introduces you to many of your favorite romance authors in a program developed exclusively for Harlequin® and Silhouette® readers.

Watch for **Romantically Speaking—Harlequin™ Goes Prime Time** beginning in the summer of 1997.

If you're not receiving ROMANCE CLASSICS, call your local cable operator or satellite provider and ask for it today!

Escape to the network of your dreams.

See Ingrid Bergman and Gregory Peck in *Spellbound* on Romance Classics.

ROMANCE CLASSICS